# Wicked Knight

## (The Wicked Horse Vegas Series)

## By
## Sawyer Bennett

Find Sawyer on the web!
sawyerbennett.com
www.twitter.com/bennettbooks
www.facebook.com/bennettbooks

# Table of Contents

# CHAPTER 1

## *Asher*

**"I** DON'T CARE what it takes to get those permits pushed through," I snarl into the phone, sitting up straighter in my chair. "If you don't have them by the close of business today, consider yourself fired."

My voice carries through the doorway of my home office, causing the chatter of the two maids cleaning the living room to go abruptly silent.

"I'll handle it," Jay Maher, my residential development manager, replies tersely. My threats aren't idle, and he knows it—just like he knows he fucked up on this deal big time.

"Yes, you will," I acknowledge quietly before disconnecting the call. I fully expect the permits to be obtained, even if Jay has to sell his soul to the devil to get it done. But that's not my problem.

Glancing at the clock on my wall, I note there's plenty of time to make my meeting across town. Punctuality is important to me. My father always says, "Respect of time will pay you back tenfold." Not sure what he means by that, but he loves to drop little pearls of wisdom on me whenever he can. When Carlton Knight retired from Knight Investment Group two years ago, our yearly gross revenues exceeded just over fifty million. When he passed on the helm to his son—and that would be me, Asher Knight—he did so with expectations I would increase that figure substantially every year.

I had no desire to disappoint him, but more than that, I wasn't about to disappoint myself. My one major failure in life rewired my internal makeup. It made success and winning the only options. So far, they have served me well.

Reaching my hand out, I brush my thumb over the framed photo on my desk. Looking at Michelle's sunny California beauty—golden-blonde hair, summer-blue eyes, and wide smile—makes me sad.

Bitter even.

I tear my eyes away because her expression sometimes mocks me. At other times, she seems to pity me.

It's rare to see her photo and feel peace or happiness, or even remember fond memories. I've realized I'm not entitled to those feelings.

She took that all away from me.

Pushing up from my desk, I grab my briefcase and exit my office. It sits just off the living area of my downtown penthouse apartment. Five years ago, I moved here after I became a widower at the age of twenty-seven.

The maids are talking again. As I enter the living room, I see one of them running a feather duster over a Chihuly vase that sits on a pedestal in the foyer. My eyes drop to her ass, which is amazing despite the wretched black polyester dress she's wearing. She's definitely new, and I know this just by looking at her ass and nothing more.

When I head into the kitchen, I find the other maid scrubbing out my refrigerator. She's been cleaning my apartment for a few years through the cleaning service I use. Her name is Gerda. She's a stout German woman who is short on words, which is fine by me.

"Good morning, Mr. Knight," she says as I head over to the coffee pot.

"Morning," I reply with a nod of my head. She sticks her head back in the open refrigerator, and I pull a travel thermos out of a cabinet to make a to-go cup of java.

Just as I'm reaching for the carafe, the explosive sound of glass breaking fills the air.

"Fuck," a woman, most likely the maid with the fine ass, screams. When I look over my shoulder, I see my Chihuly vase in a million pieces on the floor. Bits of cobalt blue, cream, and sunflower-yellow covers every inch of the marble foyer.

My eyes travel up shapely legs, polyester-covered thighs, an amazing set of tits under a ruffled white apron, and the face of a fucking goddess. A combination of high cheekbones, full lips, and golden eyes that are slanted like a cat's. They are sly and sexy. Her hair is pulled into a long ponytail the color of dark wood and cherries. My body instantly reacts to her.

"Oh my God," Gerda exclaims in distress as she bustles over to the shattered remains of my one-of-a-kind Chihuly. "Hannah… you stupid cow."

"Fuck," the beauty—Hannah—says again as she stares aghast at the expensive mistake she just made.

Her fretful gaze slides to me. She bites down on her lower lip, fear filling her eyes. Not sure what it says, but it's sexy as hell to me. I want to fuck her more than I want to chastise her.

"I am so fucking sorry," she tells me. Her language incenses Gerda, galvanizing her into action.

"Hannah," she snaps to gain her attention. "How could you be so stupid and careless? I trusted you with this job and—"

"Gerda," I interrupt quietly, but I've never needed to raise my voice to command attention. Both women turn to me, Gerda appearing slightly green. I'm sure she thinks she's going to be fired for this. "Please return to your duties. I'd like to talk to Hannah privately."

"But—" Gerda says in confusion.

"Hannah," I say, turning my back on the women. "In my office, please."

My body is tight and hyper aware as she walks in behind me. I ignore the chair behind my desk, wanting a bit less formality between us. When I pivot to face her, she doesn't have an ounce of fear on her face. She does, however, look almost as sick as Gerda did a minute ago.

"Close the door," I order, not wanting Gerda listening in on us.

She reacts immediately. After she's done my bidding, she turns and starts to blabber. "I'm so sorry, Mr. Knight. I'm not usually that clumsy. I barely touched the vase, but it wobbled. When I tried to steady it, I accidently knocked the damn thing right off the pedestal. But please don't fire me. I need this job more than you can even imagine. I'll pay you back for the vase."

"It was a one-of-a-kind, commissioned piece that cost seventy-five-thousand dollars," I inform her blandly.

"Fuck," she curses again, and I find myself liking that dirty mouth a lot. What I wouldn't give for that mouth on me.

"A payment plan then," she blurts out.

"Pretty sure it would take you the rest of your natural life... and then your children's lives, too, to pay it back," I drawl, taking a step toward her. She holds her ground. Stopping in front of her, I tuck my hands casually in my pockets.

"I work three jobs," she says as she stares up at me. Although she gives off a somewhat tough and sassy exterior, I like that I tower over her and could probably easily break her if I wanted to. "I'll make it work somehow. Please, don't fire me."

"Why three jobs?" I ask curiously, because while she

and I are nothing alike, I do admire a hard work ethic.

Her jaw tightens, and she lifts her chin in defiance. Her words are short and clipped. "I have family to take care of."

Not really of interest to me, but I like that she's desperate and part of her fate is now in my hands.

Turning away from her, I saunter over to a file cabinet that's up against one wall. "I would be amenable to you working the debt off for me."

"How?" Her tone is instantly suspicious, and it tells me she's no dummy. She probably knows where I'm going with this.

I ignore her for a moment as I slide the top drawer open. Flipping through a few vertical files, I finally find the one I'm searching for. After I pull out a piece of paper, I close the cabinet.

Turning back to her, I make my offer. "One night with me at my sex club and I'll forgive the entire debt."

Hannah blinks at me, and the most stupid thought comes to my mind. *What is her last name?* Is it sweet and innocent sounding like "Hannah," or is it filled with gumption since I sense that in her as well? For the life of me, I can't figure out why that would even cross my mind because it's of no consequence.

*She* is of no consequence other than to fulfill a fantasy I've managed to develop in the past five minutes.

Those eyes, which are just a few shades lighter than cognac, narrow at me. "You want to have sex with me in exchange for me breaking an overpriced and not very attractive piece of glass?"

"Yes, at my sex club, the Wicked Horse," I add, so she understands that requirement. I ignore her slam at my art purchase. "It's a safe environment, and I won't ask you to do anything you're not comfortable with."

"Do I look like a whore?" she snarls, teeth bared. My cock starts to fucking swell at the thought of bringing her to heel.

"Not at all," I say smoothly. "But you do look adventurous. It will be fun and incredibly liberating for you."

"Because you're basically offering to pay me for sex? By forgiving a seventy-five-thousand-dollar debt?" Her hands ball into fists, which she perches on her hips. My hands would look good on her hips, holding her from behind.

"I'm offering you a way out of an expensive predicament you just landed yourself in. I wouldn't think you a whore if you accepted. Merely an enterprising, smart woman who knows a good deal when she sees it."

I expect her to throw more indignation my way. Let's face it… I've insulted her in making my offer.

Instead, she surprises me by saying, "What if I'm not attracted to you?"

Lust flashes through me, and I prowl toward her. She holds her ground. When I'm inches away, she starts to step backward. I follow until her back comes up against the door, but stop short of touching her in any way.

Bending slightly, I place my mouth near her ear. I can feel the harsh escape of her breath against the side of my neck when I whisper, "How about this... you come with me to my sex club. We'll have a drink. Talk."

Hannah makes a sound in her throat, which could be desire or disgust, but it doesn't stop me.

"If I can't get you wet while we talk, I'll accept you're not attracted to me. Of course, it will take my hand between your legs to verify, but I'm quite sure I know what I'll find. You'll want it, Hannah, trust me. And when the night is over, you'll be thanking me."

A hand comes to my chest, and I know she can feel the gallop of my heart. She gives me a strong push backward, and I comply.

I peer down at her, not even trying to hide the slight smile of amusement I'm feeling right now.

Hannah glares at me and her words are gritted out between clenched teeth. "Thank you, but no thank you. I'm not interested."

Raising the hand holding the paper I'd pulled from the cabinet, I wave it mockingly at her before I hand it over. She has no choice but to take it from me.

As her gaze drops to it, I explain, "That's a copy of the invoice for the vase. Like I said... seventy-five grand."

Facing turning red, she mutters under her breath, "Asshole."

This makes me chuckle as I reach past her for the

doorknob. She scrambles to the side, and I open my office door.

Before I exit, I tell her, "My phone number is on the invoice. Call me if you change your mind."

"I won't," she snaps.

I give her a wink. "I bet you will."

I don't wait to see what she does. I just walk out of my office without looking back.

# CHAPTER 2

# *Hannah*

*I BET YOU will.*

Those damn words have been playing in my head all day, despite the fact I keep telling myself I'm not interested in his proposition.

Even though I am very much attracted to Asher Knight.

What sane woman wouldn't be?

Look up the word "gorgeous" in the dictionary… there'd be a picture of Asher Knight.

Put "gorgeous" in any online thesaurus, and all that would pop up would be picture after picture of the man.

It's not fair that he's just my type. Bossy, alpha, and determined. Add on the almost midnight-black hair, light hazel eyes, and what's clearly an impressive physique under that expensive silk suit he was wearing, and it took all my willpower to be affronted by his offer.

Truth is, however, I'm not offended. He made me an offer that—under normal circumstances, say we'd met at a bar or something—I might have accepted once I was able to decide he wasn't a serial killer. I have no aversion to casual, safe sex.

Not that I get it often.

Or at all lately.

And… he said it would be safe.

And I could say 'no' if I wanted.

He also implied he could get me wet from words alone. That's not a bet I'm willing make with him, because he pretty much did when he started whispering in my ear in his office.

"Agh," I mutter as I leave my last cleaning job of the day.

Grudgingly, I have to admit he saved my ass from Gerda's wrath. When I finally had the strength in my wobbly legs to walk back into the kitchen, she was waiting for me. She pointed at the glass, which Asher must have had to walk over to leave his apartment.

"Clean that up," she snapped. "And you're lucky… I would have fired you, but Mr. Knight said he worked out a payment plan and I was not to terminate you. That it was a simple mistake that could be easily forgiven."

God, I hated learning that. It made me like him just a tiny bit. Although it made me feel beholden as well, and that was something I just can't be. I have too many things on my plate that hold me hostage as it is. There are so many things pulling at me—there's just not any room to give another ounce of myself.

Snagging my phone off the passenger seat of my little beat-up Nissan Sentra, I manage to start a call to Nelson. As always happens whenever I gear up to talk with my ex, I must take deep, calming breaths while the phone rings.

He answers without any warmth in his voice, but the feeling is mutual. "What can I do for you, Hannah?"

"I want to speak to Hope," I say, hating I feel like I need permission to speak to my own daughter.

Which isn't true, of course. Nelson may have primary physical custody right now, but I have joint legal custody. There are no limitations in our divorce decree that limits the amount of phone time I have with Hope. I could call her ten times a day, which I would love to do, but that would be a little insane.

Nelson sighs into the phone. "She's not here right now."

My brow furrows. "Where is she?"

"Amelia took her out shopping for school clothes," he says, and my entire body bristles.

"I was going to do that this weekend," I say, tone vibrating with anger. "I told you that. Hope was excited we were going to have a girls' shopping trip together. Instead, you let your current flavor of the week take her?"

I think my head is going to explode, so I barely hear his mocking laugh. "What were you going to do, Hannah? Take her to some cheap discount store? Buy her twenty dollars' worth of cheap dresses? Because we both know that's all you can afford."

Tears spring to my eyes because he's right, but I blink them back. It's all I have to offer her, but Hope is a sweet girl. She doesn't care about the quality of her clothes, but rather the time spent with me doing something fun. As she's a girlie girl, she loves trying on dresses. I might only be able to afford discount, but I had set aside some tip money from my evening job to take her for a manicure, too.

Nelson leeched me dry in the divorce. I caught him cheating, told him we were over, and he ended up winning everything. It's what happens when a man's golfing buddy is a judge and said man has the wealth, power, and prestige to buy justice. Nelson got primary custody, and I get to see Hope on the weekend. I was also ordered to pay child support, which is one of the reasons I work three jobs. Since she's living with him for the greater period of the week, I have time.

But I don't begrudge paying child support for Hope's welfare, court ordered or not. She's my child, and I'll always support her.

"I'll have her call you when they get back," Nelson says grudgingly. Because I dared to end the relationship, he punishes me at every turn. I guarantee he will not have her call me. Even if he did, I couldn't answer. I'll be working at my evening job as a bartender.

I hang up on Nelson, not bothering with any further courtesy. He extended none to me, and I'm feeling beat to shit by the course of my day so far.

Before I can set my phone back down, it rings. While I'm tired as hell and really don't want to talk to anyone, I see it's the one person who is always there for me. "Hey, Mom. Is everything okay?"

"Of course, honey," she replies with a laugh. God, I love her laugh, and it makes me smile. "Can't I just call my daughter to see how her day is going?"

Sucking in a breath, I refuse to give into emotion. My mom is calling to check on her only daughter, so I do what I always do with my mom. I paint a gloriously rosy picture. In essence, I lie to her.

"Everything is great," I say cheerily. "Just got off work and heading home now."

Instead of, "I miss my daughter, my ex-husband's an ass who does everything he can to ruin my time with her, and, oh yeah… I broke a vase today worth seventy-five grand, but hey… no worries. I'll just pick up a fourth job to work and pay it off."

I don't tell her any of that because Carol Brantley busted her ass to raise me and my brothers. Now it's her time to put her worries to rest when it comes to us. As such, I've done a damn good job of keeping most of the ugly stuff hidden from her.

That includes how badly I'm failing at life. Of course, she's aware Nelson has primary custody, but that's all she knows. She doesn't have a clue it's a constant fight to get my basic visitation rights, that I have to work three jobs to support myself and my daughter through child support payments, and certainly she'll never know I gained an additional seventy-five-thousand dollars of debt today.

She's also in the dark about the fact I help my two younger brothers out with money as needed. They're good guys, but both are immature. Toby, the youngest at twenty-one and six years my junior, got a DUI a few months ago. I helped to pay for his lawyer. Frank, who is twenty-two, is struggling to cover the payments on a way-too-expensive truck he bought while working on a road crew for the State Department of Transportation. It's growing pains for my little brothers, but I'd rather them come to me than Mom because she already paid her dues while raising us.

Settling in for the drive home, I listen to Mom chatter about the mums she planted in the front yard in anticipation of fall, and how she's making a poke cake for her church's bake sale this weekend.

When I turn into my neighborhood and see my house, I notice a tow truck sitting out front. My foot hits the brake pedal, and I come to a fast stop.

My little Nissan Sentra is about to be repoed. I'd known missing the last few payments on the car and ignoring their demand letters would catch up to me, but that was the money I sent to Toby for his DUI. I thought I'd be able to catch up on the payments, but it just didn't happen.

"Hey, Mom," I say softly. "I have to go. Got to get ready for work."

"You work too hard," she replies sadly.

"Nah…" I play it off. "I like being busy."

"You're a great mom, Hannah. I know what you do is all for Hope. If you need help, you only have to ask."

"I got it covered," I assure her. "But thank you. Now, I have to go. Love you."

"Love you," she says, and I hang up.

After checking my mirrors, I execute a U-turn and head in the opposite direction from my house. My car isn't getting taken today.

I drive straight to my next job. I'd wanted to take a quick shower and grab something to eat while at home. Luckily, I keep a change of clothes in my car. I'll just have sweaty armpits and gnawing hunger for eight hours tonight while I schlep beers for drunks, but hey… at least I still have my car.

When I pull into the parking lot across the street from the bar where I work—a dive place simply called Joe's—I reach into my purse and pull out the bill for seventy-five grand Asher Knight gave me before he left for work this morning. Running my finger under the phone number at the top, I dial.

There's no way he can know it's me calling, yet he answers in a smooth voice that's filled with rich under-currents of sex and sin. "Hello, Hannah."

"I accept your offer," I say, swallowing the disappointment in myself.

I try to reason with myself about the truth of my life. I have an asshole ex-husband who unfairly has full custody, and I'm diligently squirreling away money to hire an attorney to win my daughter back. My child support obligation is non-negotiable, as is helping my younger brothers with money as I can. To make it all workable, I eat mostly Ramen oodles, or I don't eat at all. I spend virtually no money on myself, and I work three jobs. Let's not forget I have a car I can't afford, a repo man on my ass to collect, and I'm essentially now on the run to protect my transportation so I can work the three jobs needed to do all the above.

And now, I owe a man seventy-five grand.

Of these three things currently weighing me down, there's at least something I can do about one.

I can get Asher Knight's debt off me, which will be freeing.

"I want you in red," he orders, and I have no clue what he's talking about.

"Red?" I mutter.

"Red silk panties. Bra is optional. Red dress, too. Oh, and wear your hair down."

"What part about me being flat broke don't you understand?" I snap. "I can't afford that."

He ignores me. "Tomorrow night. Be at my place at ten. I'll have clothing waiting for you."

I grimace, not over his high-handed attitude, but

over the fact that I secretly love red lingerie. It looks great with my skin tone.

At least, I think it does. Hell, it's been so long since I could afford any like that I might not be remembering correctly.

"I can't tomorrow night," I say. "I have to work. But I could probably get a night off next week."

"Tomorrow night," he merely says, and it makes me roll my eyes in frustration.

"I have a job. Responsibilities. I can't just—"

"Five thousand dollars," he says, and the words cut sharp across my tirade, making me go mute.

My voice is raspy. "Pardon?"

"Five thousand dollars," he repeats. "I'm sure that will compensate for the tips you'll miss out on tomorrow night. Call in sick. I'm sure it's not a big deal."

Five thousand dollars?

Does he know what a figure like that could do for me? It wouldn't go toward my car, my brothers, or even food for myself.

No, it would let me retain an attorney to fight for custody for Hope.

I don't even have to consider. "I'll be at your place at ten."

His laugh is low and husky, causing a shiver to run up my spine. "Can't wait," he murmurs before disconnecting the call.

# CHAPTER 3

## *Asher*

I CAN'T FIGURE out if she's putting on an act, but Hannah isn't behaving like I expected her to. I figured she'd be pretty pissed I backed her into this corner, so I was prepared to deal with a sour attitude. Instead, from the moment she showed up at my door wearing jeans, a threadbare t-shirt, and perfume that smelled like cinnamon spice, she has displayed nothing but a cavalier attitude about going to a sex club with a stranger.

It tells me she has backbone, which makes her even sexier because I'll enjoy making her bend to me.

I shift into third gear, the engine of my McLaren 720S whining to be let loose, but that's not going to happen driving the downtown streets of Vegas. The skirt to the miniscule red dress I'd picked out for Hannah rides high on her legs, but she hasn't tried to tug it down once. My gaze has wandered there a time or two, and Hannah knows it.

There's not an ounce of nervousness I've detected so

far. The only thing she's shown me since we left my apartment was brash curiosity. "What kind of man forgives a seventy-five-K debt and throws an extra five thousand cash on top for one night with a woman?"

"A rich one, I expect," I reply without taking my eyes off the road. "Although I assure you, this is the first time I've ever made such an offer."

"I'm so lucky," she mutters dryly. "Why me? What's so special about me?"

Not sure if she's looking for flattery, but I'm not that great at giving it with a measure of restraint. Sure... I could growl in her ear that I love how tight her cunt is, but softer stuff isn't my thing.

So I merely shrug. "It doesn't have anything to do with special. I just like to indulge whims."

She's not offended. "Makes sense."

"I would hope so." My tone is bland. "I work hard for my money, so I enjoy the fuck out it."

Hannah drums her fingers on the top of her bare thigh, drawing my attention to that pale skin. I want to bruise it with my teeth, and I hope to fuck she returns the favor.

"What exactly do you do for a living?" she inquires sweetly.

My eyes cut back to the road. "Land development."

"What does that mean?"

"It means I buy up chunks of property and create shopping centers, subdivisions, or retail office space."

"Interesting," she murmurs, but I doubt she believes it since she doesn't ask anything more about what I do.

But I'm curious about this woman who would accept my offer of a night of sex with a stranger to forgive a huge debt. "So you're a maid and a bartender, but you said you worked three jobs. What's your other?"

"Online customer service support for a phone company," she says with absolutely no enthusiasm. And why would she? Her jobs are awful. "I pick up shifts when I have time here and there."

"What's your last name?" I ask, wincing with disappointment in myself that I'd even waste breath on such an inconsequential detail.

"Madigan," she says, turning to look out the window as I pull in front of The Onyx casino.

"We're going gambling?" she asks as a valet rushes to open her door.

"The Wicked Horse is on the top floor." Another valet opens my door. I pull a twenty out of my wallet as a tip before handing the keys to him.

"Thank you, Mr. Knight," the kid says appreciatively.

After I give him a nod, I round the front of my car to meet Hannah on the sidewalk. She looks amazing with bare shoulders, sleek legs, and her mahogany locks spilling down her back. I'm going to fist the fuck out of it tonight.

Men's heads turn because it's hard not to notice a

woman like her, and my gut burns with anger that they are eyeballing her. Pushing it down, I offer her my arm.

She takes it without thought, walking beside me into the lobby of the casino. Turning toward a private elevator with the neon Wicked Horse logo sign above it, I steer my date that way.

When we're inside ascending to the top floor, Hannah asks, "So, what exactly is a sex club? I mean… you can have sex with me at your apartment. What's so great about this place?"

"It's better if you just see for yourself, but the short answer has a lot to do with adding the excitement of fucking in front of others. You're not shy… are you, Hannah?"

She shrugs, and her tone is blasé. "No one will know me here."

Chuckling, I put my hand over the one of hers tucked into the crook of my arm. "That's the spirit."

I'm rewarded with a sly smile as the elevator doors open.

The Wicked Horse Vegas is modeled after the original, which opened in Wyoming inside a large silo. The owner, Bridger Payne, wanted a place for people to be able to let loose on their sexual inhibitions without fear of judgment or reprisal. The members of this club are kinky, sensual, and adventurous. Fucking in front of others is only half the fun, but it's the best part in my opinion.

The hostess at the podium greets me with a smile. "Good evening, Mr. Knight."

I smile back and lead Hannah around her, noticing the surprised reactions I get from some of the regulars. They've never seen me come in with a woman on my arm because it's just not something I do. Instead, I meet women here, fuck them, and then leave alone.

I usher Hannah over to a long bar in what is known as the Social Room. It's a place to meet and mingle. Perhaps have a cocktail or two if someone needs to loosen up. I don't know if Hannah needs that or not, but I'm not in a rush.

"What would you like to drink?" I ask as we step up to an empty spot. There are no stools. That way, it encourages people to move around and meet others.

"White wine," she says. "Any type. I'm not picky or savvy enough to tell good from bad."

I would imagine a woman who has to work three menial jobs wouldn't know much about the fine distinction amongst wines, but I never cared much for that stuff anyway. I'm a bourbon man myself.

I order drinks while Hannah casually takes in the scene around her. Leaning an arm on top of the bar, I cross one ankle over the other and study her without shame of getting caught ogling.

Her gaze comes to me, and she lifts her chin. "Like what you see?"

"From the moment I checked out your ass in that

horrid maid's uniform," I admit.

The bartender returns with our drinks. After I pay him, I hand her a glass of wine and she takes a dainty sip. I ignore my bourbon for the time being.

"There are different rooms here that we can choose to play in," I say. She startles slightly before her eyebrows rise in curiosity. Smiling, I lean closer. "There's the Waterfall Room where everything gets very wet. Good for oral sex as long as you don't drown yourself while you're at it."

Hannah laughs, and I like that she has a good sense of humor.

"The Deck is outdoor fucking on a clear acrylic surface that looks forty stories down," I continue.

She shakes her head. "Afraid of heights."

"Noted," I acknowledge with an incline of my head. "The Silo is intense, and I wouldn't start a newbie with it."

"Why not?" she asks with wide eyes.

"Are St. Andrew's crosses and industrial dildos your thing?" I ask playfully.

Her face flushes and she ducks her head slightly, taking a sip of her wine to forestall answering me. When she brings those lovely eyes back my way, she admits, "I don't know. Never tried either."

God, what I wouldn't give to put her on one of Jerico's fuck machines. He's got a new one that hoists a woman into the air, so she can be placed in any number of amazing positions. Put a woman upside down in it and spread her legs, and a mechanical dildo will jackhammer her from above. I would kill to watch Hannah come that way.

But I only have her for one night, and I don't want to send her running. "I think we'll start with the Orgy Room."

Her head pops up, eyes flaring wider.

"It's sort of self-explanatory." I grin.

She avoids saying anything by taking another sip of wine, this one resembling more of a gulp. I use the opportunity to slide a finger under the thin spaghetti strap at her shoulder.

Hannah freezes, her eyes pinned on mine.

"You have no idea the things I want to do to you in this club." My words are truthful. Dropping my attention down to where I'm barely touching her skin, I slide my finger out, turn my hand, and graze my knuckles over her breast. I continue back and forth a few times until I feel a nipple harden through the silk. My cock responds, thickening against the confines of my pants. "I wonder if you're wet for me, Hannah?"

"What?" she rasps.

"You said you weren't attracted to me," I murmur, reminding her about her brash words yesterday. "Were you lying to me?"

When she doesn't respond, I glance back up to her face, finding her eyes burning with something undefinable.

My knuckles travel along the underside of her breast, down the side of her ribs, and over her hip. My gaze follows its path. I give a playful tug when I reach the hem of the red silk dress I picked out for her to wear today. Lifting my head to see her face, I meet her stare head-on.

"Spread your legs a little," I whisper, taking a step into her space.

Her breath rushes out and she shakes her head, but it wasn't done with enough strength to get me to back off.

"Open your legs." I repeat it as a command.

She obeys me without question, and I move in closer.

"Good girl," I praise, bending my neck until my forehead just touches hers. I lower my voice. "Let me see what you feel like."

God, but I fucking love the way she moans as my hand inches under her dress. I haven't even really touched her, yet I can tell she's turned on. She shifts, spreading her legs perhaps a bit more for me.

My fingers reach the juncture of her legs, seeking the lacy edge of the panties I also bought for her. They were delicately made, totally see-through, and would ride high on her hips.

Instead, my fingers meet soft curls. I jerk back so I can see her face. She smirks, and I can't help the lazy smile of appreciation that spreads on my face that she disobeyed me by not wearing the panties I'd told her to. The smile curves into a wicked grin as I realize she's been naked under that dress all this time, and I now have easy access to her cunt.

Running my finger through the lips of her sex, I feel the heat and wetness that lets me know she is most definitely attracted to me.

I consider getting her off right here for everyone to see. It's not normally done... not in the Social Room, that is. But it's also not against the rules.

Hannah stares at me before giving a tiny lick of her lower lip. Her expression exudes a confidence in her sexuality. While it's clear this isn't how she prefers to handle a debt, she's enjoying what we have going in this moment.

Removing my hand from between her legs, I relish in the slight tinge of disappointment that flashes over her, then take a step backward. "Let's finish our drinks, so I can show you around the place."

Yeah... I'm going to take her into every room, introduce her to the hedonism this club has available, and then get my due from her.

# CHAPTER 4

## *Hannah*

HOW MY LEGS are even supporting me at this point is a true miracle. Perhaps to torture me or to just get me in the mood, Asher gave me a tour of the entire club. It included each room he had described except for the Deck. He was surprisingly gallant about not needling me about my fear of heights.

Within each room, I saw actions that defied imagination. The Silo fascinated me the most with its circular rooms made of transparent glass around the perimeter. Inside, people were on full display as they performed the kinkiest sexual acts I have ever seen.

Asher explained everything to me, seducing my sense of hearing right along with my sight. His voice a low, sexy murmur near my ear.

*Look at that woman right there; she's taking three men at once. It's beautiful.*

*I'd love to see you locked in the stocks—naked and at my mercy. Maybe I'd even share you with a few other men.*

*Ever been on a St. Andrew's cross before? You look like a girl who could take a little pain.*

I've never been with multiple men, or been into BDSM, but watching sure as hell made me realize there was a world out there that intrigued the hell out of me.

I wonder if Asher instinctively knew that about me. Could he peg me as a woman who would be susceptible to such things when he made his proposition?

Outside the Orgy Room, Asher stops to talk with a man who is exiting. I don't pay him any attention. Instead, I stare past both men to get a brief glimpse of what lies inside before the door closes. When it does, I'm forced to give attention to the gorgeous acquaintance conversing with Asher, who is regarding me with curiosity.

"I see you brought someone in tonight," the man says. He's as tall as Asher with blond spiky hair and a trim goatee.

"Trying something a little different," Asher says with a shrug, his hand pressed to my lower back where it's been most of the evening. His thumb strokes me through the thin silk of my dress, making my nipples harder than ever.

I don't even take offense to his disregard of me. I'm not here to make friends or be something other than a one-night stand to Asher, so it's of no consequence when the blond man gives me a polite nod and walks off.

Asher pulls the door of the Orgy Room open, then

motions for me to go ahead of him.

The glimpse I'd had before doesn't do justice to the full-scale debauchery going on inside. My breath stops as I take it all in. The room is massive, dimly lit, and furnished with a variety of low-slung couches, chaises, and even piles of sumptuous pillows to recline on.

Couples, threesomes, and even foursomes are sprawled all over, actively engaging in sex. The air is filled with a sexualized vibe, pulsing with moans, dirty whispered words, and slapping flesh. Although the room is darkened, there are spotlights in the ceiling that aim down on the furnishings, supplying stark revelation of the entangled masses below.

I'm terrified and exhilarated at the same time.

"Amazing, isn't it?" Asher asks as he takes my hand and leads me around the perimeter of the room.

Not quite the word I would use, only because it doesn't seem powerful enough.

I gawk as I follow Asher to the far side, where he brings me to a stop next to an extra-wide cushioned platform where a woman is having sex with two men.

I don't consider myself naïve and threesomes aren't a new idea—*thank you, romance novels*—but seeing it is something to behold.

One man is flat on his back, legs over the edge of the cushioned bench and feet planted on the floor. The woman is on top of the man, riding him.

Except she's not sitting up straight and proud; rather,

she's leaning forward with her hands gripping the man's shoulders. The second man stands at the edge, right behind the woman, and he's fucking her in the ass.

I'm mesmerized, taking note that the woman isn't even moving. The men are doing the work, drilling into her so she's practically delirious with pleasure.

"I can arrange that if you want," Asher says as he moves behind me. His hands come to my waist to hold me in place, not that I'd turn away from this spectacle. "Kynan McGrath—the man I just spoke to before we walked in—is a good friend. He'd be more than happy to oblige."

I shake my head. As fascinated and turned on as I am, I'm sure that would hurt like hell.

Chuckling, Asher moves his body in close to mine. I can feel the heat of his chest at my back, then his warm breath is at my ear. "Just as well. I'm not sure I really want to share you on your first visit here."

I startle at his words, not only that he's feeling proprietary, but also his implication I'll be back here again at some point.

"First and only visit," I remind him, quite breathlessly to my chagrin.

"Of course," he agrees politely. But then, his civility is gone as he moves one hand from my hip to my stomach where he presses his palm into my belly. He holds me tight, and I can feel his erection against my lower back. It's thick and hard. I have to resist the urge to reach behind me to touch him.

His other hand leaves my hip to pull my hair away from my neck. My eyes flutter closed when I feel his mouth on my skin. He grazes his lips up my neck to my ear, murmuring, "Are you turned on by watching other people fucking?"

No sense in lying, so I nod. I'm beyond turned on. Besides, he already knows it, so what's the use in lying?

Asher's hand slides down my belly to my pelvis where he uses his fingers to inch my skirt up. Panic flashes over me as I realize he's going to blatantly reveal my body to the crowd. When I lock my small hand on his wrist, he hesitates.

"Want me to stop? Or do you want my fingers in your sweet cunt?"

Air hisses out through my teeth as my body sort of melts backward into him, clearly capitulating. I let go of his wrist, snake my arm up, and wrap my hand around the back of his neck while I lean into his shoulder. I even slightly spread my legs, which makes Asher groan in approval before he slips a finger right inside of me.

He curses low. "Fucking dripping."

A shiver runs up my spine. My hips buck as he pulls out and drags the wet tip over my clit. It's so sensitized. I'm so turned on it won't take much to get me off. In fact, I want to beg him for it.

I want to plead with him to make me come, and I want to promise to do dirty things to him in exchange.

As I think all these things, I ignore the flash of guilt I simultaneously experience. I remind myself of what's important—I can use the money he's paying me to fight for Hope. What does it matter if I experience pleasure out of the deal, too?

The five thousand will hire me an attorney. Not the best, but certainly a good one I can pay to take on Nelson's high-priced attorneys.

Stars burst in my eyes as Asher presses two fingers into me, so deeply I come up on my tiptoes. His other arm wraps tightly under my breasts as he hitches me up a little further, holding me almost off the floor while he fondles between my legs with touches so sinfully on point that my blood starts to rage.

"Please," I manage to rasp out, and he laughs darkly.

He doesn't make me beg any further, though. Twisting his hand, he uses his thumb to strum my clit. The feeling of his fingers inside me and the pressure on my nub—the way he's got my dress hiked up so he can obscenely finger fuck me in front of a room full of people—it all has me reeling.

Before long, I'm breaking apart as I start to orgasm.

"Yes," he growls in triumph as my muscles clench onto his fingers. A low, rumbling moan of release escapes my lips.

Then his hands are gone, and my dress is being tugged over my head. My arms willingly lift, giving him lazy access to bare my entire body, and then he spins me around.

Lowers me onto a mound of huge pillows covered in dark purple silk that must have been there the entire time, even though they seem to magically appear so we have a soft bed of iniquity for our use.

He towers over me, eyes roaming over my body as he starts to disrobe. I blatantly stare at him, still immersed in a haze of post-orgasmic bliss and burgeoning new lust as his clothes come off.

Asher's cock is enormous, veined, and beautiful. I wonder if he wants my mouth there. I'll gladly do it.

Instead, he's kneeling between my legs. Awestruck, I watch as he rolls a condom onto his hard length. His hands go to my legs, pulls them further apart, and then he lowers himself onto me. I sink further into the plush pillows, feeling completely captured by the weight of his body.

The tip of his cock is pulsing at my entrance, but he doesn't move. Instead, he stares at me a moment before lowering his head to place his mouth on mine. It's the first time we've kissed.

He's made me orgasm… and we haven't even kissed yet.

Just as his tongue sweeps into my mouth, he presses himself into me. One long, sliding sweep of his cock into my pussy. When he's fully impaled, he lets out a soft groan into my mouth.

I had thought having sex in front of a bunch of

strangers would be as embarrassing as it was titillating. Instead, all thoughts and reason just seem to melt away.

As of now, there's only Asher and me in this room. I'm completely consumed by the way he feels inside of me. When he begins to move, I start to fly. His thrusts are so fully penetrating, so demanding and consuming, that I find my body giving over to him completely. Another orgasm fires, brews, builds, and with a deep thrust from Asher, breaks free. I buck and scream. He kisses me harder to smother it.

Fucks me harder.

His hands go to my wrists, and he pins them above my head. Fierce lust in his hazel eyes, Asher gazes at me. I start to burn from the inside out. Another tremor of pleasure hits me hard, runs up my spine, and has me arching into him.

"Fuck," Asher grunts as he plows deeply into me once more. As he starts to come, I watch the veins stand out at his temples and his eyes flash with relief as he pours himself into the condom with a massive, heaving shudder of his body.

Staying stiff for a moment, he finally relaxes and slumps against me. It's for long enough that I can bring my hand to his head and run my fingertips through his sweaty hair. I almost have time to open my mouth to tell him how amazing that was before he's rolling off me.

Asher stands, grabs my discarded dress, and drops it on my legs.

"It's getting late," he says as he peels the condom off and tosses it in a nearby trash can.

Nabbing his pants from the floor, he reaches into a pocket and pulls out a piece of folded paper. He hands it to me. Numbly, I take it while holding my dress over my lap.

I thumb the paper open, knowing exactly what it is.

A check made payable to me for five thousand dollars.

# CHAPTER 5

## *Asher*

AFTER HAVING BEEN gone on a business trip the last three days and having just disembarked the redeye from Los Angeles to Vegas, I really should be heading home for a good night's sleep.

Instead, I leave the airport, turning not toward my downtown luxury apartment but rather to a local bar called Joe's. My assistant easily obtained Hannah's second place of employment along with the address, which I put into my navigation system. It's in an area of town that's not quite used to seeing a three hundred-thousand-dollar sports car, and I worry slightly it might get boosted. I hope the car alarm is enough to dissuade some would-be criminal, but it's hard to tell.

It's not a worry that's big enough to thwart me, so I park in a darkened lot across the street. Besides, it's why I have insurance.

When I open the bar door, I'm hit with a wave of smoke and realize I must be obsessed with Hannah. Why else would I come to this stinking pit when I could easily just call her?

When I spy her behind the bar, pulling a mug of draft beer, my body tightens with need. It's all it takes to have my answer.

I simply want her again, and I want her more than my common sense should allow.

Music from a jukebox blares, forcing the patrons to scream to converse, and the air is hazy with smoke. I grimace as I wind my way through a light crowd of early drinkers—it's only about nine—and make my way up to the bar.

Hannah doesn't see me. Once she serves the draft beer to a customer, she turns and asks the next person what they're drinking. There's another female bartender working at the other end, slinging drinks as fast as Hannah.

It's busy and decidedly not glorious work. Hannah is tipped a pittance for her efforts, but I can tell she tries to make it up in serving volume, efficiently moving from customer to customer.

When she finally glances my way, there's a curt smile on her face that she has in place for everyone. Her mouth parts to ask what I'm drinking before she fully gawks at me in shock.

"Hello, Hannah," I say in a voice loud enough to rise above the din as I tap my finger against the scarred wooden bar top.

"What are you doing here?" she asks, equally as loud as she positions herself directly across the bar from me.

I jerk my head toward the door. "Can you take a break?"

Hannah stares at me a moment, clearly undecided. Here she stands in a dirty, smoke filled bar, looking amazing in a tight tank top with tattered daisy duke shorts, and I don't think I've ever been more attracted to a woman before.

She holds a finger up to me to say she needs a moment, then walks to the other end of the bar. Her head inclines toward the other bartenders. They exchange words, then Hannah is headed my way. Pushing away from the bar, I walk to the end to meet her at the pass-through. After she exits, I escort her to the door that leads out, my hand on her lower back. It's completely reminiscent of the way I escorted her through the Wicked Horse five days ago.

When I had what was the absolute best sex of my life.

Which sort of blows my mind and freaks me out at the same time. It was nothing over the top. Totally vanilla—outside of the fact we were in a sex club—but Jesus... how many women have I fucked missionary style in my life?

Too many to remember... and so many occasions that were forgettable.

But Hannah has opened something inside of me that I didn't even know existed. While it scares the fuck out of me, it's too intriguing for me to ignore it.

I push the door open. My chest brushing against Hannah's shoulder shoots a ripple of pleasurable awareness through me. She continues, and I wonder if she's as affected by that touch as I am.

I follow her to the corner of the building, far enough away from the door that we can have some privacy from customers going in and out.

She turns, faces me, and pushes her hands down into the pockets of her jean shorts. Tilting her head quizzically, she asks, "What's up?"

She doesn't say, *God, I missed you.*

*Will you take me back to the Wicked Horse?*

*Thank you for the best sex of my life, Asher.*

Fuck, I need to quit thinking those thoughts. I absolutely do not want Hannah beholden to me in any way, and that includes having an insatiable need for sex from me. Because I'm afraid I'd be too weak to resist that temptation.

Okay, that's a lie. I would not say no to that, which is proven by the fact I'm standing here in front of her.

While I'd rather just kiss the fuck out of her, possibly pull her to the side of the building and fuck her up against the wall because I'm insanely turned on being in her presence right now, I decide to play it cool. "I want another night with you."

Just as I expected might happen, her cheeks glow pink with embarrassment, which turns me on even more.

Her expression turns bewildered. "Why?"

"Because I enjoyed fucking you, Hannah," I reply matter-of-factly. This is, after all, really a business deal. "And I think you enjoyed it, too. So I'd like you to be my companion—"

"Your companion?" she exclaims with a mirthless laugh. "What does that even mean?"

"I want you to be available to accompany me to the Wicked Horse on certain nights of my choosing," I tell her.

Hannah just stares at me, her eyes turning blank for a moment before she bursts into laughter. "Your sex companion? Tell me you're joking."

I lean into her and murmur, "I never joke about sex. And I'd pay you well to accompany me there."

She blinks, and there's an iciness in her tone that wasn't there before. "You want me to be your full-time whore?"

Through my locked jaw, I grit out, "I never used that word, nor would I ever. But if it eases your conscience, you are free to tell me 'no' at any time we are inside that club. It will totally be your choice."

Hannah crosses her arms under her breasts, which pushes them up against the low cut of her tank top. I refuse to let my gaze drop there.

"Let me get this straight," she says with a hefty dose of suspicion. "You want me to go with you to a sex club in the evenings, for which you will pay me money. And if I don't want to have sex with you, I don't have to."

"That's the gist of it," I mutter.

"You don't think I have the power to say no to you, do you?" she accuses with her lower lip stuck out. It makes me want to bite it.

Even though that's exactly what I think, I don't admit it. Instead, I just stare at her.

Wait her out.

Finally, she sighs and drops her arms. "Doesn't matter, anyway. I work nights at Joe's, so I can't be your *companion.*" She holds up air quotes to emphasize her offense at the word. "I can't give this job up."

In my mind, I thought it would be cool if I could have access to Hannah a few nights a week. I figured that would appease this insatiable need for her that I've developed somehow. But now a different sort of thought takes hold.

"I'll pay you double whatever you make at all three of your jobs combined. If you quit them, then you're available to me."

Hannah's mouth drops open into a perfect "O," and I have a clear fantasy of what I'd like to see filling that space one evening.

As if she could read my lewd thoughts, she narrows her eyes. "You'd pay me double what I'm making at all three of my jobs, just to accompany you to the Wicked Horse on some evenings where I have the right to say 'no' to your advances?"

My lips curl up in an evil grin. "No. If I'm going to pay you double what you're currently earning, I expect you to quit all three of those jobs and be at my beck and call, not on 'some' evenings, but 'all' evenings."

Hannah worries at her lower lip, her gaze casting off to the side as she thinks.

I add gravy on top. "I'll give you a fifteen-thousand-dollar signing bonus up front."

Her gaze slams back into me, eyes wide with surprise. "Awful lot of money for a whore," she murmurs.

Fuck... I just actually made her a whore if she accepts this. But I press on.

"Again, your word, not mine. Besides, you can—"

She beats me to the punch. "Say 'no'. Yeah... I heard you. But if I say yes, then that makes me a whore."

She sounds glum, and I wonder if it's because I've basically given her a guilt-free way to accept this deal or maybe because she doesn't have the willpower to say no to me.

"How about I hire you as my full-time house manager?" I add, hoping to add some legitimacy to the offer.

"What the hell is a house manager?" she gripes.

"You'd manage my home. Keep it clean, well-stocked, make meals, handle my dry cleaning. Stuff like that."

"And go to the Wicked Horse with you."

"We could stay in at my apartment some nights," I say with a mischievous grin.

She doesn't smile back.

Instead, she gives me an apologetic grimace. "As much as that sounds like an amazing deal for any woman, I'm afraid I'm going to have to say 'no'."

The emphasis she puts on the word 'no' isn't lost on me. She's showing me that she has resolve.

I step into her, causing her to back up against the dirty stucco exterior of the building. Putting my hands near her head, I dip my head so my face is near hers. "You're being stubborn, Hannah. But I like it."

Her mouth curves in amusement.

I bring my lips near her ear. "Besides… I'm quite confident you'll change your mind."

She snorts, and her hands go to my chest to push me away from her. Giving her a wink, I turn to leave.

I look left and right as I walk away, considering it safe to cross the road back to my car. Holding my hand up, I wave at her, knowing without even glancing back that she's staring at me.

Raising my voice slightly, I say, "Call me. I'll be waiting."

"Don't hold your breath," she yells, and I chuckle.

Yeah… she'll change her mind.

By the time I get in my car and start it, Hannah has already disappeared into the bar. A message notification comes up on my dashboard screen, which is synced to my phone through Bluetooth. I press a button on my steering wheel. After a soft tone, I say, "Play voicemail."

There's a short pause as I back out of my parking spot, then I hear my father's voice. "Asher, call me. I think you're making a mistake on the Tyndall property. There's no way you'll get investors to bite at it. It's going to fall flat, and you'll look bad. If you look bad, Knight Investment Group looks bad. So call me."

Rolling my eyes, I press the button on my steering wheel to delete the voicemail. I make my way back toward the nicer part of town to my apartment. As I drive, I consider what to say to my dad when I call him back, and have no doubt, I will call him back. No one disregards a summons from Carlton Knight.

My dad and I have always had a strangely unusual relationship. He's arrogant, self-centered, and ruthless when it comes to business. I've been told by many that I'm just like him, but perhaps a tad more ruthless.

We get along fine because our worlds are centered around making insane amounts of money. When my father passed on the mantle of CEO of Knight Investment Group to me, it didn't mean he was going to keep his opinions to himself. It means nothing to him that I've doubled our wealth and holdings since I've taken over. He's still going to give me advice whether I want it or not.

He's lucky I usually want it, because I respect his entrepreneurial acumen. It doesn't mean I'll always follow it. Regarding the Tyndall property, I'm absolutely going with my gut instinct on this. It's the one significant difference between us. I'm willing to take risks he never would have in business, and it's hard for him to understand that about me.

Regardless, I respect the man greatly, which means he still has tremendous influence over me.

But I choose not to call him back tonight. I don't feel like butting heads with him. It will totally ruin my surprisingly good mood after spending just moments in Hannah's company.

Instead, I call someone who is usually a pleasure to talk to.

My twin sister Christina.

She answers on the third ring with an affectionately irreverent greeting. "What's up *Ash-hole*?"

"You know, after twenty years, that nickname is a bit overused," I reply drolly.

Christina's laugh is husky and mischievous, and it sounds just like our mother's laugh, which causes my chest to ache. While I'm everything like my father, Christina took after our late mother. She's kind to everyone and focuses all her free time on philanthropy.

Like me, she's ivy-league educated—I went to Penn, and she went to Yale—but she disappointed Father and forever endeared herself to Mother when she decided to become a public-school teacher.

"Are you back in town?" she asks as she munches on something crunchy, which crackles loudly over the phone connection.

"Just flew in a bit ago. Headed home now. Just thought I'd check in and see how you're doing."

"I'm good," she replies with more crunching in the phone. She does it to annoy me as only a good little sister—younger by almost three minutes—can do. "Met with the venue manager this morning, and everything is a go."

I smile. "That's good. Need me to do anything?"

"Got it covered," she replies, which makes my smile wider. She's like Dorothy Knight incarnate, able to put on a charity gala that will cater to the Vegas wealthy elite, yet be relaxed enough to crunch on whatever the hell she's eating while she talks about it.

And this is no small affair. It's been renamed in honor of our late mother—the Dorothy Knight Charity Extravaganza for the Benefit of Children's Hospital. There will be over one hundred in attendance for a dinner that costs one-thousand-dollars a plate to raise money for the hospital. It was a project my mother was passionate about, which my sister took over without any hesitation.

"Listen," she says after swallowing her food loudly— also to annoy me. "I've got someone who would be perfect for you to take to the gala. She's a new teacher at my school, and she's—"

"Forget it, Christina," I say curtly before she can get another word out. "I'm not interested."

"But she's so sweet and really pretty. I think if you—"

"I said forget it," I say with a little more bite than I'd intended. Christina is the person I love most in this world. I don't like to hurt her, but I also don't want her overstepping her bounds. She can get a little crazy with her notions of wanting me to find love again.

"Asher," she says quietly, a slightly chiding tone to her voice. "It's time to move on."

Ignoring her, I wrap our conversation up. "Listen... call me if you need any help and I'll be glad to step in."

She sighs into the phone, sad I won't talk to her about the most terrible and horrific thing to ever happen to me. My sister wants me to move on, but how can I get over the fact that my wife killed herself and it's all my fault for not stopping her?

"I'll talk to you later," I mumble, then disconnect the phone before I start feeling too guilty for cutting my sister out. I know she loves me and only wants to help, but I don't want her to be disappointed in the fact I can't be fixed.

Nor do I want to be.

# CHAPTER 6

## *Hannah*

I PULL UP in front of Nelson's house, a red-tiled, five-thousand-square-foot stuccoed monstrosity that he kicked me out of when I asked for a divorce. Which was fine. I never liked its formality anyway. There was too much blank space to feel cozy.

Still, it irritates me just a little that he continues to live in splendor, has my daughter almost exclusively, and takes child support from me, not because he needs it but because he wants me to suffer.

None of that compares to the bitterness I must swallow daily when I think of the way I got hosed in Hope's custody hearing. My attorney was decent, but I could have had the best in the world and it wouldn't have mattered because the judge was one of Nelson's golfing buddies. He tried to make it seem like he fairly considered all the facts but when he awarded full custody to Nelson, granting me weekend visitation with alternating holidays, I knew that the judicial system was anything but unbiased.

When it boiled down to it, Nelson's connections, money, and influence swayed the court, not what was in Hope's best interest.

It's been hell watching him raise her with me having so little say in what happens in her day-to-day life. Our moments together are so fleeting. It makes me feel like she's slipping away from me.

It's unbearably frustrating that my economic situation is what is holding me back from playing on a level field with Nelson.

My mind drifts briefly to Asher and his incredibly ridiculous offer, and there's a moment of wistfulness as I consider what that bonus could do for Hope and me.

Pushing that out of my head, I turn the rearview mirror my way to take a quick peek at myself. I didn't get home from work until about three AM, and I couldn't get to sleep weighed down by my worries about Hope and Asher's bold offer to be his "house manager".

Ridiculous.

I sigh, disregarding the black circles under my eyes and the fact I didn't even bother to put on makeup this morning to cover them up. Pushing the mirror back into place, I get out of my car, taking only my keys with me.

After I lock the car, I cross over Nelson's perfectly manicured lawn to the large portico. I trot up the steps, ring the doorbell, and step back to wait for him to make his way through the cavernous house to greet me.

Sometimes, I'll hear the patter of Hope's feet as she races to the door in excitement to start our short weekend together.

Right now, I get nothing but silence.

I ring the doorbell again.

When no one comes, I finally hit the button repetitively, hearing the gong of the bells inside over and over again.

Nothing.

"Fuck," I curse under my breath, stomping off the porch and back to my car. I unlock the passenger door, reach into my purse, and pull my phone out, angrily tapping on the screen to pull up Nelson's number.

I dial him, and he answers in a breezy tone. "Hello?"

"Where are you?" I growl. "I'm here to pick up Hope."

"She's on a camping trip," he replies with a smirking undertone. "I texted you about it yesterday."

"You did not text me about it," I grit out, my voice quavering with fury.

"I did," he insists, and I can see the smug look on his face in my mind. If he were here before me, I'd claw it off him. "It's not my fault you've got a shitty phone. It probably didn't come through or something, but when I didn't hear back from you, I just assumed it was okay."

"You are an asshole," I screech. "You know I wouldn't have agreed to it. I get so little time with her, and I would not have let her go."

"She really wanted to, Hannah," he chides me. "You know, it's not all about you. You have to let Hope do stuff without you."

My body starts shaking over the unfairness of what he's saying—as well as the little bit of truth within.

Sucking in a breath, I let it out slowly. "Fine. Then I want her on Monday and Tuesday night to make up for it."

Nelson laughs through the phone. "What are you going to do, Hannah? Have her sit up at the bar while you serve drunks?"

My free hand balls up into a fist, and I squeeze my eyes shut. I can't even fucking have my kid on a weeknight because I have to work to be able to support her. It's fucked up and incredibly unfair.

Tears spring to my eyes. I blink furiously to battle them back. It doesn't work, and they slip down my cheeks.

"Listen," Nelson says dismissively. "I've got to go. But I'll make sure to tell Hope when she comes home tomorrow that you don't want her to go on any trips with friends in the future. I'm sure she'll love you for that."

"Don't you dare," I hiss, but all I can hear is dead air.

The asshole hung up on me.

"Goddamn motherfucker," I scream as I turn and slap my hand against the hood of my car. The shock reverberates through me, causing my bones to ache.

The anger starting to swiftly turn to depression, I make my way around to the driver's side and throw myself into the front seat. Just as I start my car, a text chimes through. I have an insane thought that perhaps Nelson has had an attack of conscience and is reaching out to make things better.

When I look down at my phone, I'm hit with another punch of despair to my gut.

It's not from Nelson, but from Toby, my brother.

*There's a Fender guitar at a pawn shop that's an incredible deal. Can you loan me $200?*

A maniacal laugh comes unbidden, and I think I might be cracking up under all this stress.

From the weight of all the things pulling at me.

*No*, I write back.

It's a short, curt response from me, and he quickly responds. *No worries. Thanks anyway.*

He even puts a kissing face emoji.

I had a hand in raising Toby and Frank because my mom worked herself to the bone to be able to afford rent, utilities, and food. She waited tables at a honky-tonk bar in rural South Carolina where the pay was horrible and the tips even worse. I admire the hell out of her for it.

I toss my phone back in my purse, then head back across town to my house where I suppose I'll spend a lonely day laying on my couch watching sad movies.

I'm strangely blank as I make the fifteen-minute

drive, refusing to let my mind obsess over my shitty situation. If I had to put a name to the numbness starting to creep through me, I might even label it as "giving up".

"It's okay," I tell myself gently. "You can give up this hard fight. No one would think badly if you did. It's not winnable anyway."

Maybe I should give up. Move away. Hope might be better off without such a mother in her life. What could I possibly give her? What lessons could I even teach her when I can't even support her or myself?

I come from a family that has always slogged through hard times. Perhaps I should move back to South Carolina to live with my mom. There's no shortage of bartending jobs there.

I'm beyond mired in depression by the time I pull up to the curb bordering the small, dusty front yard that is my abode. It's in a terrible section of town, but the rent is affordable, which is all that matters.

I dejectedly haul myself out of my car, so lost in my own misery I don't hear the vehicle pull up behind me.

It's not until someone says, "Excuse me… are you Hannah Madigan?" that I snap out of it and turn that way.

My stomach cramps as I see an overweight man heading toward me from the tow truck that just pulled up to the curb. He's carrying a clipboard. Even though I don't acknowledge his question, he goes on to say, "I'm here to take your vehicle."

Just fucking great.

I snatch my purse out of the car, then set it on the hood. Without a word to the man, I get in the backseat, unlatch Hope's car seat, and yank it free. After I set it on the ground, I close the door with a bump of my hip before angrily removing the car key from the key ring. When it's free, I toss it at the repo man. It's an unexpected move, and he drops his clipboard as he tries to catch it.

I don't look back at him, though. Instead, I grab my purse and the car seat, then move across my yard to my house.

Yes, it would be so easy right now to just give up on everything.

Instead, as soon as I step over the threshold and close the front door behind me, I call Asher.

He answers, not with smug anticipation but rather a guarded question. "Have you changed your mind?"

"I have," I respond smoothly and with a confidence that shocks me since I was contemplating throwing in the towel just moments ago. "I accept your offer on the condition that I have weekends off."

"That wasn't part of the deal, Hannah. I want you at my beck and call, and that means whenever my fancy strikes me."

"Then find another 'house manager,'" I say with quiet sarcasm that I should bear such a ludicrous title.

"Because I need weekends off. It's non-negotiable."

I'm not giving up one more minute of my time with Hope, and I'm going to use that crazy signing bonus to hire an attorney first thing on Monday. I'm going to fight Nelson for joint physical custody, and I'm not going to stop until I succeed.

Even if that means I have to suck Asher's cock Monday through Friday.

Although I grudgingly admit it doesn't really sound like a chore to me.

Regardless, I have a new plan of action. I'm going to make this work for Hope and me.

He's quiet, and I panic for a moment that the deal might be blown. My mind scrambles to find a middle ground with him, but it's not needed.

Asher's words are nonchalant. "Be here at eight AM on Monday."

"I'll be there," I clip out with a modicum of geniality in my voice. He is my employer after all. "But I need to have Monday afternoon off to take care of something personal."

"Fine," he mutters. "But you're going to the club with me Monday night."

"Fine," I snap.

"Fine." This time, he adds a low, sexy laugh. "Maybe we can work out some of that aggression you seem to be harboring right now. I like a little rough, angry sex. Don't you?"

A shiver tickles up my spine at the prospect. My sex life wasn't overly adventurous with Nelson, so I have no clue if I like it rough or not.

Something tells me, however, that I'd probably like anything Asher offers, so I throw caution to the wind by taunting, "Do your worst, Asher."

"Be careful," he warns in a low growl. No doubt he wants to strip away any fake aura of confidence I might be trying to fool him with. "I'm of the firm belief that pain enhances pleasure. I can't wait to teach that to you."

My brain fuzzes up a bit at the prospect, an ache forming between my legs. While I have no clue if I would even like such a thing, my body clearly is interested in the concept.

I have no idea what I've gotten myself into with this man, but there's no turning back now.

As of this moment, he's the key to getting my daughter back.

# CHAPTER 7

## *Asher*

I SHIFT INTO third gear, only blocks from the Wicked Horse where I told Hannah to meet me. My entire body is buzzing with anticipation, and I'd be lying if I said part of that wasn't nervousness.

It's not an emotion I'm used to feeling as confidence is my middle name and borderline arrogance is my game. And it's not Hannah herself who has me apprehensive.

I mean, she twists me up for sure, but I can handle her.

What has me on edge is how much I want her. It borders on being out of control, and it's not something I'm used to.

Today has dragged by. I could barely concentrate at work, which was not a good thing since I was negotiating the Tyndall property, which my dad seems to think will be a failure. I was able to get my head out of my ass long enough to seal the deal, but then I was off thinking about my upcoming night with Hannah.

It had been that way since she showed up at my apartment at eight this morning, just as we'd agreed. I shouldn't have been surprised she showed up in shorts and a t-shirt as September gets hot in Vegas. She had on a pair of comfortable, if not overly worn tennis shoes, and was carting a bucket full of cleaning supplies.

I opened the front door when she rang the bell, took her all in, and asked, "What's with the bucket?"

She rolled her eyes, and my palm tingled with the strong urge to spank her. "You did say you wanted me to clean your apartment, right?"

"Right," I say. In actuality, I had totally forgotten that whole "house manager" shit I threw at her to ease her conscience. I made a mental note to call the cleaning company I normally used to cancel their service.

Hannah didn't need any instruction on how to clean my apartment as she'd done it before, although I warned her not to break anything else. When I got another eye roll, I had to bite back a smile.

I gave her a credit card for any purchases she'd need to make, told her my grocery preferences, and how I like my shirts starched from the dry cleaners. She also said she would make dinner for me each evening. She was apparently taking the "house manager" role seriously as she was the utmost professional as we talked.

That was fine. I let her have her moment of aloofness, knowing she'd melt under my touches tonight.

Before I left for the office, I told her, "Meet me at the

Wicked Horse at eleven. There's a parking garage attached. Just give your name to the attendant there. He'll put you in a private spot near the door."

Hannah shook her head. "I don't have a car, so I'll be taking an Uber."

"Why don't you have a car?" I asked, knowing it was none of my business and I shouldn't care.

She shrugged. "It was repoed yesterday."

I had a million questions. How could a woman working three jobs not afford a car payment? Why was she so blasé about the fact she'd lost her transportation? And most importantly…

"That's why you accepted my offer?" I hazarded a guess.

Her eyes glittered with amusement. "It was one of a long list of reasons."

Damn my fucking curiosity. "What was the top reason?"

"That's my business," she replied primly. Without another word, she walked away from me, heading toward the kitchen to start cleaning.

I hadn't liked her having the last word, and besides… there was one more thing I needed to handle with her. I followed her, watching as she unloaded cleaning supplies onto the counter.

"I want you to get on birth control." As expected, her mouth dropped open in shock, questions filling her eyes. So I explained. "I want to ditch the condoms."

"I'm on the pill," she stammered.

I nodded, glad to know I was close to being able to fuck her bare. "And you'll need to get tested for STDs."

Her face turned cherry red. "Excuse me?"

"Get tested. I'll do the same today. You can put it on my credit card, since I assume you don't have any health insurance."

Hannah shook her head, a blank expression on her face.

"If you don't have a regular doctor, you can see my primary. I can get you an appointment."

"I have a doctor," she muttered, her head ducking down to inventory her supplies.

"And you can use my other car for any errands you need to run on my behalf." She didn't look back up at me. "Keys are in the drawer of the foyer table. It's the white Mercedes G550 in the garage, and the gate code is 9556."

"Okay," she murmured, still refusing to look at me. Laughing, I'd turned to walk out with one last parting shot. "There's a box for you in my room. Wear it tonight."

I had the briefest glimpse of her head shooting up and her eyes trying to lock with mine, but I gave her my back and sauntered to my door.

What would she think of the dress I'd bought for tonight?

Knowing I'm about five minutes away from seeing

her in it has my groin starting to tighten, and I barely get my McLaren to a stop in front of the valet stand before I'm jumping out.

I shove the keys and a twenty at the attendant, who meets me at my door, while ignoring his "Enjoy your evening, Mr. Knight". My eyes search the crowd lined up to get inside. When I don't see Hannah, I make my way into the lobby.

And holy fuck… when I see her, I'm struck practically dumb. The dress I bought is indecent, and it couldn't be worn anywhere but a sex club. It's nothing more than strategically crisscrossed strips of black patent leather that barely covers her most private parts. A three-inch shiny black swath cuts across her tits, wide enough to hide the areola in its entirety and thick enough I can't see her nipples. It's tight enough that it plumps them up with deep cleavage. Two diagonal straps crossing over her flat stomach attach to a wide piece that wraps around her crotch and ass. It barely covers her pussy. If I were to look at her from behind, I know it would expose the bottoms of her ass cheeks.

I bought the dress knowing it would make her uncomfortable. I want her off balance. But I also know it will make her feel sexy and goddess like, since I'm sure she can see the reverence for the beauty before me on my face.

She stands with her legs a few inches apart, one hip slightly cocked. A pair of black sandals that have a wide strap around each ankle with a tiny jeweled crystal dangling from the buckles encase her feet. Arms hanging loose and relaxed, she grips a tiny clutch purse in one hand.

Her face, though… that's different. She went heavy on the makeup with dark, smoky eyes and a deep plum stain on her lips. Her hair is a riot of waves, appearing as if she just stepped inside after spending a day on a windy beach.

I saunter up to her, my eyes roving all over her body. I don't see an ounce of discomfort on her face, making me wonder if she's putting on a brave face to take away some of my joy in her innocence to all of this.

When I reach her, I lift a hand and rub my thumb over her bottom lip. Her breath rushes out, warm and sweet. Glancing at the pad of my thumb, I'm happy to see a purple smudge from her lipstick. I intend to have it all over my cock later.

"I like this color," I say gruffly.

Hannah smirks. "I bet you're just wondering what it will look like all over your dick, right?"

"Guilty," I admit bluntly.

"Typical," she replies, and I throw my head back to laugh. She's not nearly as uncomfortable as I thought she'd be, and she has a dirty mouth on her. I like that because she's showing me she has grit, but that just makes me rise to the challenge even more. I bet before the night is through, I'll have her blushing all over.

"Shall we?" I ask, holding my arm out gallantly.

Hannah tucks her hand in the crook of my elbow, and I escort her to the elevator that will take us up to the Wicked Horse.

Once inside, I release her hand and move mine to her lower back. It's warm, and I intend to have my mouth there later. Everywhere really.

"How was your day?" I ask, watching the digital numbers tick higher as the elevator ascends.

"It was fine," she murmurs. "I was even able to get into my doctor today for a blood test."

My heart slams inside my chest. "Did you get the results yet?"

"Tomorrow."

Well, shit. But all good things come to those who wait. Still, I feel compelled to inform her. "My doctor rushed mine and I'm good to go. As soon as you get yours, let me know."

"Yes, sir," she says tartly.

"I like you calling me 'sir,'" I reply darkly, dropping my hand down to her ass. I slide it low, pushing my fingers across bare skin—I knew she couldn't possibly have panties on under that miniscule amount of leather—and right between her ass cheeks.

Yelping, she tucks her ass under, but I'm not deterred. Pushing through the warmth straight to the tight opening, I press the tip of my middle finger there.

She lets out a harsh breath, her body swaying into

mine. I chuckle, leaning slightly into her. "My cock is going to love your ass."

She shakes her head violently. "No fucking way."

"We'll see," I say nonchalantly and pull my hand away, only to take hers back again. I squeeze it briefly, and we both watch the numbers ascend until we reach The Wicked Horse.

When the doors open, I pull Hannah from the elevator, walking briskly through the lobby after nodding to the hostess at the podium. I'm well known by everyone and don't need to stop to check in.

"Aren't we going to have a drink first?" Hannah asks, practically trotting to keep pace with me.

"Not in the mood." My reply is terse, and I take a slight left once I make it past the double doors that lead out of the Social Room.

Down a hallway and into the Waterfall Room.

It's a sinfully opulent room with a circular, heated pool in the center. In the middle of that, a waterfall cascades from the ceiling onto a platform about fifteen feet in diameter. It pours through a crystal chandelier that has long ropes of colored prisms hanging from it.

The flooring of the room is textured cement done in black with silver sparkles and inset colored stones. Along the perimeter are couches and chaises done in shimmery vinyl that can handle wet bodies and bodily fluids. Attendants dressed in black wait in the darkened wings of the room, ready to swoop in to discreetly clean the furniture off as needed.

On the far side, silvery satin curtains frame a double-glass doorway that leads outside to The Deck. This is an area that's off limits, since Hannah's afraid of heights and I don't want her fainting or getting sick on me.

"I'm thinking you naked on the middle of that platform, with my face between your legs," I say in a low voice, and her small hand wrapped in mine jerks with surprise. I tighten my hold, pulling her along.

"Wait," she exclaims, the tinge of panic in her voice making my cock start to thicken.

I don't answer her or slow my pace.

"Wait," she growls and jerks her hand away, planting her feet in place.

I turn to face her, an amused smile on my face. "Surely you're not pulling the shy card on me, Hannah."

Her chin lifts proudly. "No, but you're moving just a little fast. This is all a bit… intense."

"Which is what makes it exciting, right?" I taunt.

She turns her head left and then right, taking in the scattered couples and threesomes lounging around.

Kissing. Fondling. Fucking.

When she looks back to me, she says, "I just thought we'd ease into things before you put me on center stage with a spotlight shining down on me."

An idea comes to mind as I regard her nervously chewing on her lower lip, her arms now wrapped protectively around her stomach.

Crowding close, I put my palms against her cheeks and force her to look at me. I nod toward the platform in the center of the pool. "You are going to be on center stage there tonight, and I'm going to gorge on your pussy while everyone watches. But perhaps we can have a little fun foreplay before that, maybe off in the shadows to start."

Relief fills her eyes, and she gives me a grateful smile. Dipping my head, I press a hard, fast kiss to her mouth.

Then I have her hand in mine again, and I'm leading her to a curved loveseat tucked into a dark corner. When I reach it, I release my hold on her, turn to face her, and plop down onto the cushion. She stands before me, her head tilted in question.

I lean back, spread my legs, and start working my belt. Giving her a lecherous grin, I nod toward the floor. "On your knees, Hannah. Let's mess up that pretty lipstick of yours."

Her warm eyes flare wide, then heat up, which I find immensely gratifying. Whether it's because she's attracted to me and really wants to suck my cock or because she's grateful I'm not going to start out in the center of the room where everyone can see us, she drops gracefully to her knees right between my legs. Her hands, oh so warm and tentative, come to rest on my thighs. My muscles leap under her touch as I work my pants open, pulling my fully hard cock out. I'm eager for her mouth.

Hannah's eyes are locked onto mine for a moment

before her gaze slowly drops down to where I'm now stroking myself. She licks her lower lip, and a groan tears free from my chest.

"Give me your mouth," I order, the gruffness of my voice giving away the lust brewing hotly within me.

Her hand slides up my thigh and takes hold of my dick. My balls cramp just from the warmth of her touch, then my eyes roll into the back of my head when she leans forward and licks the tip.

I let my breath out slowly, seeping it through my teeth in a silent hiss. My body goes lax as she takes me into her hot mouth and when she moans, causing vibrations to run down my length, I pray to God I don't blow my load like a schoolboy.

Feeling brave, I open my eyes, staring down my body at her beautiful head bobbing over me. I touch her hair, sift my fingers through it, and gently grip the back of her head lest she think to pull away. Punching my hips up, I take way too much satisfaction in the slight choking sound it produces from her, but then I settle back and let her set the pace.

And after I come down her throat, I'm going to put her on that platform in the middle of the pool. I'm going to make her come over and over again, and then I'm going to fuck her hard for the whole goddamn club to see.

And when I'm done with that, I'm going to take her to another room and fuck her again.

Probably once more after that.

If my estimation is right, I won't be able to get enough of her.

# CHAPTER 8

# *Hannah*

I SAVE THE dusting of Asher's apartment as the last of my chores for the day. It's sort of a nostalgic thing for me, since it was my dusting of his Chihuly vase that landed me in his bed.

Or rather, in his sex club.

We've not been on a bed yet.

Couches, pools, and pillows, but not on a good old-fashioned mattress.

I wait for a flush of shame to hit me, but that's happening less and less when I think of my current situation. Perhaps I've just tucked it away into a box and placed it in a far corner of my mind, or perhaps I just don't care anymore because I've got a good opportunity to get custody of Hope now. However it boils down, I can't bemoan a situation where I'm working less hours, making more money, and having enough extra to fight for my daughter.

The attorney I hired is going to file a motion with

the court to reconsider the terms of custody and child support. He wants me to have at least a month of employment under my belt at my new job. Of course, I didn't tell him "house manager" was just a term used to mean "sex toy," but I was confident that would never be an issue. Asher put me on his payroll, and I'm having taxes taken out. I had to fill out a W-9 and everything. He even went as far as to offer me health insurance, which I wasn't idiotic enough to turn my nose up at.

Of course, all these things happened after our night together in the Waterfall Room at The Wicked Horse, and they happened via email and text. I haven't seen Asher since then.

There was no explanation as to why he hasn't asked me back to the Wicked Horse, and he's been gone to work each morning by the time I've arrived at his place. He'll usually leave me a handwritten note of what he wants done. If he doesn't, I just clean the same areas I'd cleaned the day before. Asher has what must be the cleanest abode in the state of Nevada.

I start with his bedroom, an area of the apartment that affects me the most because it smells just like Asher. It's decorated in black and gray with just tiny hints of white. It's stark and barren, but it's decorated just like the rest of his apartment. There are no personal photographs of his family, nor any warm or whimsical pieces of art adorning the walls. The black lacquered furniture is austere, but at least it shows any dust that might dare to have accumulated since I cleaned the previous day.

I make short work of his room and the spare bedroom, moving past his locked private office he instructed me to ignore my first day. The kitchen has already been scrubbed top to bottom, so I head into the living room. When I finish that, I turn to the foyer, which has a small table on one side of the door and the white marble pedestal that used to house his Chihuly vase before I broke it.

I see something laying on the top of it I hadn't noticed when I let myself in this morning. As I get closer, I see it's a photograph of something I recognize at once.

The wooden stocks that are in one of the glassed rooms of the Silo, which is one of the sub rooms within the Wicked Horse.

I pick it up and study it. There's no one in the room and certainly no one locked in the contraption, although I'd seen it in use on my first visit there. A woman had her head and wrists enclosed as she was being fucked from behind by a man. That hadn't been shocking, but the fact there were four other men lined up after him to take a turn had been. I was horrified and turned on at the same time, which made me feel like a total slut that any part of that would appeal to me. I guess it was knowing the woman was enjoying herself, which clear by her moans and screams of pleasure, that had made it seem tantalizing.

Shaking my head to clear it of those thoughts, I turn

the photo over. Near the top, Asher had written *Tonight at ten*. Under it was another short message: *Enjoying this far more than the Chihuly*.

A snort of amusement involuntarily pops out of my mouth, and I clap my hand over it. Given my observations of Asher's apartment and the fact the Chihuly was about the only color he had in here, I'm going to take a guess and say that the vase had some special significance to him. What that could be, I can't imagine, but it makes his words a little more shocking that he's liking sex with me better than his custom-made vase.

I simply don't know what to make of it.

I will have to admit that the two nights I went to the club with him were by far the best sex of my entire life. Of course, my earlier experiences were limited to my first boyfriend, who I lost my virginity to, then Nelson, and then one guy after him who just wasn't a good match on any level. None of them even understood what foreplay was, and I was lucky if I could manage to get myself off with my fingers whenever Nelson was humping me with no finesse. Our sex life was something I truly hated about our marriage. I hadn't known how to make it better, and I never felt comfortable enough to talk about it with him. I was always afraid of hurting his feelings or something.

Asher on the other hand?

He is sex incarnate. He embodies everything that is lust and pleasure. He's beyond adventurous and totally confident in whatever he does. When he commands me, I'm powerless to say no.

We were in the Waterfall Room on Monday. Every night since then, I've gone to bed thinking about it with my fingers playing between my legs. The orgasms I gave myself were soul shredding as I repeatedly replayed in my mind how satisfying it was to suck his cock, or how wanton and liberated I felt when he put me on that platform in the middle of the pool and buried his tongue deep inside of me. I came so fast I couldn't quite understand what had happened, and he continued to mercilessly suck and lick at me until he drove me to another orgasm, then another, before he finally fucked me.

And when he fucked me, he did it by putting me on my hands and knees and driving into me with almost a brutal sense of determination. He pulled my hair, slapped my ass, and pinched my nipples so hard they bruised, but I kept begging him for more.

Face flushed, I shove the photo in my pocket. Using the feather duster, I attack the marble pedestal and try to drive those memories out of my head. If I don't, I'm apt to go lay myself across Asher's bed and get myself off. I'd then wipe my wet fingers on his black satin duvet cover and wonder if he'd smell me later.

"Ugh," I growl out in frustration. I can't stop thinking about him or the sex we have, and it worries me.

It worries me that he has a power over me that has

nothing to do with the ridiculous amount of money he's given me and will continue to pay me to be his fuck toy.

"Stop thinking about it, Hannah," I chastise myself out loud, hoping it makes a bigger impression on my conscience.

A text chimes on my phone, and I nab it from my pocket. It's my mother, and her words are just what I needed to make me smile. *Thinking of you. Know you are loved.*

Carol Brantley was dealt a hard life from the moment she was born in Gaffney, South Carolina to a deadbeat dad and an alcoholic mother. The oldest of five kids, she had to go to work at the age of thirteen to help support the family. She didn't graduate high school, ending up pregnant with me shortly after she'd turned seventeen. My dad left as soon as he found out he'd knocked her up. I've never met him. My mom was unlucky in love a second time, too, and married Toby and Frank's dad. He left shortly after Toby's birth, so it was just the four of us. My mom raised three kids on a bartender's salary.

To say life was hard is an understatement, but it's also molded me into a hard-working woman with grit and determination. I started working when I was just twelve—after school and in the summers—to help with the family expenses. It was usually cleaning the neighbors' houses or raking leaves to earn a few bucks here or there. Every little bit helped, and I routinely contributed to buying groceries, school supplies, and thrift store clothes for my brothers and me.

I was determined to break the family tradition, though. After I graduated from high school, I went to community college for one year. But then I met Nelson, who was attending a conference in Columbia while I was working part time at a coffee shop there. He swept me off my feet, and I jumped at the chance to run off to Nevada with him. I was just nineteen when we married. Not a day goes by that I'm not guilt ridden for leaving my mom and the boys behind, but my mom was happy for me. She wanted nothing more than for me to pursue my dreams.

I text my mom back. *I love you. You're my hero.*

She replies with a heart emoji.

It doesn't take me long to finish dusting the foyer, and I leave a note for Asher on the counter that says, *See you at ten.*

By the time I'm walking out of his apartment and locking the door behind me, I'm making a mental calculation of the time I have left in the day. I was going to work a four-hour shift this afternoon doing customer service support, which I can do from home. I did not quit that job as the hours are flexible. Since Asher wasn't keeping me busy all day, it was a good way to pick up a little extra cash that I stashed in a Christmas pot I would use to buy Hope something special.

Instead, I decide to go car hunting. The daily Uber charges to get to and from Asher's apartment, as well as to The Wicked Horse, are adding up. I'm sure I can get a cheap used car for a lot less than what I'm spending on Uber and far less than getting my repoed car back. I only had to put down a five-thousand-dollar retainer for the attorney to take the case, which was the original bonus Asher had given me. The lawyer will require another five thousand to file the motion, so that'll leave ten grand in my savings account. I figure I can get a car for hopefully less than half. I consider it a wise investment, especially since I'll be getting Hope tomorrow. The last thing I want to do is pull up in an Uber at my ex-husband's house. I don't want to deal with the humiliating remarks he'll make when he learns my car has been repoed.

Yes, I have a good plan of action today. After I go car hunting, I'll work a few hours doing customer service support from the comfort of my own home if I have time this evening. Then I'll get showered, put on the red dress I wore on my first night at the Wicked Horse, and meet Asher there—where I'll let him lock me up in the stocks to do God knows what to me.

I'm not sure whether I should hate myself or not, but I'm looking forward to it.

# CHAPTER 9

## *Asher*

M Y FATHER HOLDS his drink up, the amber-colored bourbon lit up from the candle burning on the table. "Great job on the Tyndall deal."

I hold my drink up. "Thanks."

We sip and share a meaningful congratulatory smile. The waiter appears, returning my credit card and the receipt for me to sign, which I do after adding a hefty tip.

"You continue to amaze me," he says, but not necessarily with beaming pride in his son. It's more in an incredulous way, like he can't believe I pulled off something he would not have dared yet again. And that's because no matter my achievements and the fact I continually make this company more successful each year, he just doesn't want to believe I'm as good as or better than he ever was. His ego won't let him.

When I do a quick check of my watch, I note it's closing in on nine-thirty. I need to get going. Got a hot night planned with Hannah and the stocks.

"Your sister seems to have the gala well organized," Dad says nonchalantly, but I can hear the faint tone of ingrained disappointment in his voice. Even though I make him envious of the things I've accomplished, my father has never disapproved of me the way he does Christina.

She's the epitome of everything our mother was. While my father was fond of his wife and loved her in the best way he could, he expected both his children to be like him.

Christina's first major failure was in taking her ivy-league education to become a public-school teacher. Her next was in giving away most of her trust fund to charitable organizations. The killing blow was in marrying a man who had no greater ambitions in life than to also be a public-school teacher like his wife.

As such, my dad and sister don't have much to do with each other. He wasn't much of an influence on her growing up, anyway, not the way he was on me.

But the one thing he will always support her on is the charity gala she has taken over putting on each year since our mother died. He buys one of the insanely expensive dinner plates, and always brings some ridiculously young, sexy woman with him as a date. He'll even give a speech on how proud he is of her accomplishments with the money that's raised each year, and then after the event is over, he'll go back to ignoring her.

It's something that used to bother me, and I've had words with my father over the years for not trying harder with his daughter. It was Christina who finally told me to give it up. Not because it is a losing battle, but because she doesn't feel like she is missing out on anything. My dad has never been a doting father—to either of us, actually—and she truly doesn't feel any loss. She accepts dear old Dad for what he is, but then again, so do I. Although, I've just now stopped being incensed with him on my sister's behalf and only at her insistence that I do so.

Still, I use the opportunity to get my digs in at my dad by laying my praise of Christina on thick.

"As always, she's done an excellent job with the gala. But she's also doing some amazing volunteer work with high-risk students. Mom would have been so proud of her."

My father grunts as he stares down into his drink glass, merely an acknowledgment he heard me, but not agreeing with me. "Christina could be so much more."

"She's more than either of us," I retort, feeling a wave of anger and protectiveness for my twin course through me.

"Now that's simply not true," my father says with a smirk. "Running a multimillion-dollar-a-year company is a bigger accomplishment, and you know it. Your sister is a failure."

"I'm curious," I say in a silky-smooth mocking voice.

"Do you feel yourself to be a failure since I've made this company infinitely more successful than you ever had when you were at the helm?"

I didn't expect to cow my dad, but I'm surprised when he comes back swinging. "You're better because Michelle died. All your rage and guilt have been funneled into your work, and it's yielded positive return. I was hamstrung with a wife and kids, but you're free to give all your attention to Knight Investment Group."

For a moment, the man who was once a little boy who idolized his dad is crushed he would say something so cruel. Then I'm infuriated because I gave him an opening to strike deeply at me. I let the bastard exploit my weakness, and he's right... I had so much rage and guilt over Michelle's death, and I still struggle with it today.

But it's something I hold privately, and I'm not about to let him know he's struck a nerve.

"Always a pleasure seeing you, Dad," I murmur, with enough sarcastic bite to the word "dad" that he understands my respect of him ends where his parenting abilities start.

When I push up from the table, my father doesn't say a word. Saying nothing else, I give him my back, winding my way through the maze of tables to the exit.

Once outside, I inhale deeply of the dry desert air, letting my lungs expand to capacity before releasing it. Deep breathing has become therapeutic to me over the last few years. After I found Michelle's lifeless body on our bed with an empty pill bottle clutched in her hand and an empty liquor bottle on the floor, I went through a period where I started having anxiety attacks. My gut instinct was to self-medicate with bourbon, but Christina—who was the only person I ever confided to about what was happening to me—suggested I see a doctor. I was given the choice of medication versus meditative and breathing techniques. I chose the latter, and it ultimately worked for me.

I don't get anxiety attacks anymore but when I get pissed, I find the same tricks seem to work.

Taking in another breath, I think of Hannah. I imagine her locked in the stocks, naked and totally under my control.

My breath stutters out, and I imagine Michelle, lying on the bed with open, vacant eyes. Her expression so blank I could not discern anything from it.

Like why she did it and how in the fuck had I not seen it coming?

Squeezing my eyes shut, I conjure forth the image of Hannah again, forcing myself to fall into my fantasy. I concentrate on the smooth lines of her body as she's bent over, neck locked tight in the stocks. When I inhale, I don't smell desert heat but the muskiness of her pussy. I imagine sinking into her from behind, and I fucking force Michelle into hiding.

When I feel like I'm in control once more and

Michelle can't taunt me any further tonight, I open my eyes and turn toward the valet stand to collect my car. Grounded again, I have a firm grip on the fact that my life has room in it for a few important things.

Knight Investment Groups—which I will continue to pour my energies in to make it more successful than anything my father could have imagined—my sister Christina—who has all that is left of my heart—and hardcore, dirty, impersonal fucking at the Wicked Horse.

♦

I'VE MADE MYSELF stay away from Hannah all week, reasoning it would be better if I abstained. Like the sex would be better if I waited for it. Anticipated it a bit more.

I also wanted to set the tone with her, which is that she isn't necessary to me.

Oddly, I haven't been to the Wicked Horse since I was there with her last. That's odd because I would normally avail myself of the club at least two or three times a week, but for some reason, I was content to just wait a bit for Hannah. I'm admittedly intrigued by her, and there's no denying my body responds to her in a way it hasn't to any other woman in a long, long time.

But now that I'm here with her, in the glassed room inside The Silo with the stocks just sitting there waiting to entrap her, I wonder why the fuck I wasn't doing this with her every goddamn night. I must be insane or a glutton for punishment.

Hannah stares around with nervous eyes, her teeth worrying at her bottom lip. She's wearing the red dress she wore the first night, and it's an amazing color on her. I make a mental note to buy her more red lingerie.

We're the only ones in this room, but I left the door unlocked in case someone wants to join us. It's typical protocol in here, because most that use The Silo are into group sex. At the least, we'll attract a crowd who will watch as we fuck. The thought of displaying Hannah for everyone to admire has my cock aching already. The Orgy Room that first night, and the Waterfall Room the second, were good introductions for her, as they were dark and more intimately lighted.

The Silo is bright, open, and without privacy walls. Everything is on display in here.

"I'm scared," she blurts out. For a moment, I experience a sensation I haven't felt in years.

Empathy.

Ignoring it, I shoot her a sinister smile before walking over to the stocks. The contraption isn't authentic, since traditional stocks imprisoned people by their feet. This one was made for the sole purpose of bending someone over so they can be fucked from behind, whether it be a man or a woman. This one sits bolted into two heavy wooden beams, the top and bottom portions opening with a heavy-duty cast-iron hinge on the side. There's a larger hole for the head, and two smaller ones on the side for the wrists. To accommodate the variances in people's heights, the imprisoning part can be cranked higher or lower.

I lift open the top board, gesturing to it. "Come over here."

Hannah walks slowly toward me, despite what I recognize as a tinge of fear in her eyes. I admire her courage, but I also get off on her being a little afraid.

Still, I remind her, "You can say no."

She nods in understanding. "I won't."

Thank fuck.

"What are your hard limits?" I ask as she comes to a stop before the stocks.

Twisting her neck, she gazes out the main glass wall into the interior of The Silo before turning back to me. Already, several people have meandered up to the edge to watch us.

"No anal," she says bluntly.

"Just my cock... or can I put something else in there?"

Flushing, she lowers her eyes. "Your cock is too big."

"We're going to work up to that," I assure her, but then I give her some peace of mind. "But tonight, I'm mostly interested in your pussy, especially since we don't have to use a condom."

As expected and equally hoped for, our mutual visits to the doctor revealed we were both safe. Of course, I felt the need to make sure she understood she wasn't to fuck anyone else. Oddly, she didn't ask the same of me, but maybe she just assumed I wouldn't—which is the truth—because I was the one who wanted the tests in the first place.

"Anything else?" I ask, starting to get impatient in my need to lock her under my control.

Hannah's eyes harden slightly, her chin lifting. "No other men can touch me. Our deal doesn't mean you can share me."

Now, I'll never admit it to Hannah, but I have no intention of sharing her. Truthfully, I don't see that ever changing. I've gladly taken part in group sex before, wanting to experience every bit of hedonism that was available to me. It's the best kind of dirty fucking. While I'm all about pushing boundaries and living this life to the fullest and freest, I don't want any other man touching Hannah. I consider her mine alone.

But that's not something I will ever share with her, so I merely say, "I'll respect that, but maybe I'll get you to change your mind one day."

"Don't bother trying," she warns. "I won't."

I don't argue with her because it's moot. While I'm fucking her, no one else is, and that's that.

"Take your dress off for me," I say, lowering my voice an octave. It's not intentional, but because I'm starting to succumb to the insatiable need for her that's been brewing all week. I still need to feel in control. To prove this is my show and not hers, I order, "Then go stand in front of the glass. I want everyone out there to see what I have in here."

Her cheeks burn, pink spreading across the bulging top mounds of her breasts. Sucking in a breath, her eyes glaze over a little.

Just as there are things I'll never admit to Hannah, she'd never admit to me that's she's liking what's going on right now. I've realized she's got a bit of exhibitionism within her.

Yes, I'll start her in front of the glass. Probably have her play with herself; maybe even make herself orgasm before I lock her up.

Then I'm going to have my way with her for an exceptionally long time tonight... and I fucking dare Michelle to creep back into my thoughts.

# CHAPTER 10

## *Hannah*

I SIP COFFEE from my travel thermos as I drive to Nelson's house to pick up Hope for the weekend.

I'm utterly exhausted from last night at The Wicked Horse with Asher. We left at a reasonable time, but my body was well-used and the adrenaline rush of what we'd done had sapped my strength.

Asher took his time with me while I was locked in the stocks, and the experience was electrifying.

It was equal parts degrading and uplifting.

I've never come so many times or as hard before in my life.

From the moment he ordered me to me stand in front of the glass wall and masturbate for a crowd of strangers, I knew my sex life had been irrevocably changed because I got a rush out of what he made me do.

There was an absolute liberation in obeying his order, knowing that but for his command I wouldn't have done it at all. True... I could have said 'no'. He's made that clear often enough.

But it's also true I enjoy my time with Asher. He's awakened a wicked streak I never knew existed within me. I've run on auto pilot for so long, struggling to make it through a day working back-breaking jobs, all for just a few peaceful hours with my daughter on the weekend, that I had forgotten what it was like to experience pleasure. I'd forgotten what it was like to do something satisfying purely for myself, and that is not something I expected to get out of the deal I made with the devil named Asher Knight.

He rode me hard from behind while I was in the stocks, but not before he had me give him a blow job in front of the voyeuristic crowd watching us. With my head held tight in place by the stocks, he fucked my mouth without restraint, pulling away before he came on my tongue. He then moved behind me, driving in hard and deep.

My only regret from that experience was I couldn't see his face that first time he entered me without a condom on. He let out a harsh grunt of satisfaction when he sank inside of me—a sound that made my toes curl because it sounded like nothing had ever felt better to him.

I know it felt amazing to me, which was why I was surprised when he pulled out just before he orgasmed and came all over my back instead. It threw me off for a moment, since he is the one who wanted to do away with the condoms. I expected the greater intimacy would have been to come inside me, but when he was done, he said something that caused my skin to prickle.

He said, "I've marked you. Now everyone in here knows your mine."

His voice was low, and he wasn't speaking to me. He was murmuring to himself, and I'm not even sure he knew he said it out loud.

After, when he'd cleaned me off and released me, he was as distant as he usually is. Asher knows how to put a wall up fast, and I expect he's got emotional intimacy issues, which is absolutely none of my business.

But then he did something odd.

He insisted on driving me home rather than packing me off into an Uber. Even though I'd bought a little used Honda Accord earlier that day, I chose not to drive just in case I had a few drinks at the club to help loosen me up. Socializing with a glass of wine wasn't on Asher's agenda, though, as he took me straight to The Silo and the stocks.

Asher didn't talk much on the way to my house, and he made no comment about the crummy neighborhood I lived in, nor did he walk me to the door like a gentleman would after a date.

But he did sit out in front of my house, not leaving until after I'd shut and locked the door behind me.

I didn't know what to make of it, and I don't want to make anything of it. That was then, and this is now.

It's Saturday morning, which means I get Hope until midday on Sunday.

Despite my lack of sleep, I'm completely energized about seeing my daughter. Last weekend, Nelson let her attend a camping trip which took away one of my designated days with her. While I never would have denied her the opportunity to go if she'd asked me, I was still blaming Nelson for my loss. I think that's because I know he relished in the pain it caused me, but today is a fresh start.

Nelson has no idea I'm going to fight him for Hope. Now—thanks to Asher and his unique offer of employment—I'm going to have the financial means necessary to get my daughter back.

When I pull into Nelson's driveway, I'm surprised to see Amelia waiting on the front porch with Hope, who has a pink, sequined book bag on her back and a white stuffed unicorn with a rainbow mane clutched in her arms. She and Amelia are sitting side by side on the top step, but I barely have the car in park before Hope is shooting off the porch. By the time I exit my car, my daughter is there and throwing her little body into my arms.

"Hey, Monkey," I say with an unbidden quaver to my voice. I hug her hard while she presses her face into my stomach. At five and a half years old, she likes to show me what a big, independent girl she's become, so when she lets down those defenses and melts into me, it absolutely overwhelms my emotions. "I missed you."

"I missed you, too." It comes out muffled with her face still pressed into my middle. When she squeezes me harder, I notice Amelia has joined us in the driveway.

I give her a polite smile because out of the string of women Nelson has dated since we divorced over a year ago, she's actually the nicest of them. She seems to genuinely like Hope and makes an effort with her, although I'd prefer Nelson not have his girlfriends around as much. It's confusing to Hope that he runs through them so quickly.

Just as I know it's still confusing to her that she must live with her dad and only gets to see me on the weekend. Every time we're together, it kills me when she begs to move in with me full time. It's absolutely soul crushing when I have to tell her it's not possible.

At her age, she doesn't understand the politics of bitter divorces and she has no clue that money can indeed buy almost everything. It was certainly my lack of money that caused me to lose her. How can I explain to a child that justice can be bought?

"Nelson had to run some errands this morning," Amelia offers, I guess in case I'm insanely curious as to where my ex-husband is.

I'm not. I'm actually relieved he's not here as every time we see each other, it's a confrontation. So instead, I brighten my smile. "No worries. Thanks for waiting with Hope."

"Sure," she says genially. There's even a little bit of relief in her voice that I'm being nice to her. I bet Nelson has fed her full of a bunch of lies about what a miserable bitch I am, but whatever. She gives a playful tug on Hope's ponytail. "Bye, Hope."

"Bye," she replies, not even bothering to look at her. She instead tips her head back, clearly over the moon to see her mother, and it overwhelms me with gratitude.

"Let's go," I murmur as I ruffle her hair and open the driver's door. She hops in, scrambles over the console, and settles into her car seat in the back. She's big enough to put the seat belt on herself.

"Why do you have a new car, Mommy?" she asks as she starts to buckle herself in.

I'm not about to tell her about my money woes, so I grin. "I liked this snazzy red color. Makes me feel sassy when I drive it."

Hope giggles, accepting my reasoning.

When I see she's securely fastened in, I sit in the driver's seat and close the door. I glance at Hope in the rearview mirror as I put my own seat belt on and start the car. "What do you want to do today? The sky is the limit for you. We can go clothes shopping, or to a fancy lunch, or even bowling. Whatever you want today, we're doing it."

Hope's face scrunches with concern. "But how?"

"How?" I ask as I twist in my seat so I can see her. "What do you mean?"

"Daddy says you're poor, and you don't have the

money to take care of me," she replies with all the innocence of a child who doesn't understand those are bruising words to me.

Not that I'm poor or that my daughter knows it, but that her father would demean me to her that way. She doesn't have to say it to me, but I bet her father has also made sure she realizes she can't live with me because money is an issue. He's already teaching her that he's a better parent because he has money and I don't.

Gritting my teeth, I try to keep my voice neutral. I refuse to talk badly about her father, no matter the provocation, but I also gently correct her incorrect perception as best I can. "That's not quite true, honey. I don't have as much money as Daddy, but I have the ability to take care of you."

Hope tilts her head. "Then why don't you? Why do I have to live with Daddy? I want to live with you."

My chest constricts, and it feels like I might die as the pain in my heart is so awful. Blinking back tears, I give Hope as confident a smile as I can muster. "I know it's hard to understand, but it's not just up to me. If it were my choice, you would live with me every day for the rest of your life, any future husband you might acquire be damned. He'd have to get used to having his mother-in-law in residence."

Hope's expression turns confused, so I reach back and pat her on her leg. "I want you to live with me, and I'm going to work hard to make that happen, okay?"

She nods and grins. "Okay."

"Until I can make that happen, I want you to know that I love you more than anything in this world and I will always be there for you, whether you're at my house or Daddy's house, okay?"

"Okay."

"Now… what do you want to do today?" I ask.

She ponders a moment, letting her gaze drift up to the car ceiling before grinning at me with a twinkle in her eye that I don't often see.

"Can we just hang out at your house?" she asks. "Maybe bake some cookies, make a fort in the living room, and watch movies. We can wear our pajamas and have a junk day."

*Junk day.*

My favorite tradition with Hope. It's where we eat the worst of all junk foods and lounge around like bums, which includes watching movies, doing crafts, or even just talking about silly things like which *Paw Patrol* pup we'd want with us if we were stuck on a deserted island.

I say Chase because he could catch food with his contraptions, but she says Skye because she could just fly us off the island in her helicopter. Yes, my child is smarter than I am.

"Okay," I say with a nod, more than okay with this plan. My kid doesn't want fancy lunches, to shop for pretty clothes, or to go bowling.

She just wants to hang out with me, and I can't think of a single thing in my life that could be better.

# CHAPTER 11

## *Asher*

I PICK UP my mug, then finish the last of my coffee. It's my second cup, but not my last. I have a slight caffeine addiction.

Glancing at the clock on my desk, I wonder when Hannah will arrive. I chose to work from home this morning for the sole purpose of seeing her, if only for a few moments.

Really, I only need a glimpse. Just a few words. Perhaps reassurance that she's still committed to this job. I'm more than a little pissed she has weekends off and beyond frustrated I couldn't spend the last few days playing with my new employee at The Wicked Horse.

Oh, I tried to play at the club without Hannah, but that didn't quite work out liked I'd hoped. I spent a few lonely hours there Saturday night, finding that not one woman or orgy in progress interested me. Everything looked… dull.

Uninspiring.

I left frustrated and went home, jacking off to thoughts of Hannah before I went to bed.

I spent Sunday afternoon over at Christina's hoping good food, football, and conversation would at least keep my mind occupied. Normally any time spent with my twin passes by in what seems like a matter of moments. Our bond makes it so we never have a lack of things to discuss, but Christina could see I was preoccupied. She asked me about it a few times, and I had to lie to her. When I said I was mired in a complex property swap, she seemed to accept it.

Outwardly, that is. Inside, my twin knew I was lying but didn't call me on the carpet in front of her husband, Jack. She'd never call me out about anything in front of someone else because we always have each other's backs.

Now, she'd totally do it in private and has on many, many occasions. Even though I often don't want to hear a damn thing critical she has to say to me—especially if it involves all the ways I've changed since Michelle died—I always respect that her love for me is what causes her to care so much. Which is why I can tolerate my sister's antics.

For example, Christina invited a "friend" over to eat with us on Sunday. And by friend, I mean a beautiful, single female who was incredibly outgoing, intelligent, and engaging.

I made it almost through the third quarter of the game before I faked an important business text that necessitated an emergency trip into the office. Christina's friend bought it, but my sister did not.

She followed me out to my car and "called me on the carpet". "Come on, Asher. What could possibly be wrong with Simone? She's perfect, and you should ask her out."

"Not interested," I'd muttered as I unlocked my car, refusing to engage in this age-old debate.

I tried to open the door, but Christina leaned her entire body against it, stubbornly crossing her arms over her chest. Her look was pointed and concerned. "It's been five years."

"Not lost on me," I gritted out. "You remind me often."

"Because I love you and want you to be happy again."

"I am happy," I pointed out. "Incredibly happy being single. Why can't you accept that?"

Her smile was sad when she stepped away from my car, making a sweeping motion with her hand that told me I could leave. Her last words struck me hard. "Because I know you, and you are not happy. What you are is protecting yourself. It's going to make you miss out on something amazing one day."

When she paused, I leaned in to kiss her on her cheek. "I love you for caring. But please… stop trying to push me in a direction I don't want to go."

"Never," she assured me, and I couldn't help but

laugh. God love my sister, but she'll always think she knows what's right for me. If she had a clue I channel any loneliness I might have into a sex club, she'd flip out. It's something I won't be sharing with my twin.

The sound of my apartment door opening shoots a bolt of intense awareness through me at the thought Hannah is walking into my domain. I grab my coffee cup and push up from my chair, heading toward the kitchen.

There she is, already with the dishwasher opened so she can unload it.

And why in the fuck Hannah Madigan looks better than anything I've ever seen merely wearing jeans and a cotton t-shirt is beyond me. In my social circle, women dress radically different from her. During the day, my peers wear Chanel and Gucci. At night, they wear expensive silk and leather.

But Hannah is one of those women who's just blissfully unaware of her beauty, so much so it makes her more attractive. It's one of the reasons I obsessed about her this weekend, which is a stark and quite painful reminder that she has intruded just a little too deeply into my life.

This pisses me off.

I mean… I'm pissed off at myself, not her. She can't help being who she is, but I sure as fuck can do something about the way she affects me.

The first order of business is to take a little control

back from her, although she has no idea she took it from me in the first place.

"Why are you so late?" I ask as I stroll into the kitchen and head straight for the coffee pot.

Hannah jumps, putting a hand over her breastbone. "You scared me. And how can I be late when you never set a starting time for me?"

"Most people know a standard work day starts at eight," I reply, which is the lamest of all comebacks. I'm aware she does not have normal work hours, since I have her working until the wee hours of the morning at The Wicked Horse. Still, I feel like being an ass, so I'll be an ass. I need it to remind myself she does not control me.

She gives me a slight bow of acquiescence. While her words are apologetic, her eyes are filled with challenge. "My sincere apologies, Mr. Knight. It won't happen again."

I grunt in acknowledgment, realizing she's not going to let me win this little war of words because she fully understands I'm being ridiculous. Also, I'm assuaged slightly just by seeing her.

By being in her presence.

Refilling my cup of coffee, I say, "I'm working from the house today."

"Understood, Mr. Knight," she shoots back, giving me another smart-ass bow.

When I glare at her, she smirks back. I make sure to turn away quickly before she sees my lips curl up, because it's clear she knows how to manipulate me. She realizes if she's bad, I'll want to spank the shit out of her, which is something I did plenty of the night she was in the stocks.

She enjoyed it, but she knows I enjoyed the fuck out of it, too.

For a moment, I consider fucking her now, but that does breach the boundaries we've set. Besides, I have more control over myself than that, no matter how much I lust after her.

♦

IT'S A RELIEF when I'm able to get lost in work for a while. Back-to-back phone conferences helped, then I spent a glorious hour responding to emails. In that time, I didn't think about Hannah once.

That lucky streak ends when she walks in through the open doorway of my office, carrying a carafe of coffee. One of those insulated thermos types I didn't even known I owned. Probably something Michelle bought that had made the move with me to this apartment I'd bought after she died. I simply couldn't stand being in our marital house, surrounded by the homemaking stamp she'd put on it.

"Made you some fresh coffee," Hannah says as she strolls right up to my desk and sets it down. No cream or sugar, but then again, she watched me pour a cup of black earlier in the kitchen.

"Thank you," I tell her.

When Hannah smiles, it causes my pulse to skitter. Jesus, that a woman's smile can cause a physical reaction is disconcerting.

I turn my gaze back to my computer screen, but my entire body tenses when Hannah asks in a somewhat tight tone, "Do you have a girlfriend?"

My head snaps her way, and I narrow my eyes. "What?"

She nods toward my desk, right to the picture of Michelle. It was taken before we got married. I think we were in New York City for some function or other. It was a candid shot out on the streets. Smiling, she appeared radiantly happy.

Except now I have to wonder if Michelle ever truly was happy.

"She was my wife," I reply curtly, clearly implying I'm unamused over her curiosity into my personal life.

"Oh," she says with confusion. "Was?"

"She's dead," I state flatly.

"Oh my God," she exclaims, but then claps a hand over her mouth. When she removes it, the sympathy in her voice is unbearable to me. "I am so sorry."

My voice is flat in return. "Why? You didn't know her."

If she's taken aback by my rudeness, she doesn't show it. Her expression stays sorrowful, and her words make me feel like I'm touching a live electrical wire. "I'm sorry because it must have caused you pain."

There's a tiny part of me that's sorry for what I'm about to do. She doesn't deserve to feel the brunt of my rage, but it is indeed rage I'm overwhelmed by. Anger and fury at Michelle for doing what she did, with equal parts directed at me for not being able to save her. And there's even a tiny bit directed at Hannah for bringing this shit up.

My inability to control these feelings is something I've struggled with over the years. The only thing I can do in moments like this is reassert my control of the situation. It's the only way to overcome feelings of vulnerability, which I detest.

I let my gaze slide nonchalantly back to my computer screen, but I lace my voice with pure steel. "I want you at The Wicked Horse this Saturday evening. There's a special event I want you to attend with me."

I'm being truthful. Jerico is unveiling a new sex machine he had specially made, and I'm more than anxious to see it. Can't wait to put Hannah on one of the specialty toys in the club.

"Sorry," she demurs with her hands now gently clasped in front of her. "But I can't work on the weekends. I told you that."

"You can have Friday off in Saturday's place," I tell her with a magnanimous nod of my head.

"No," she replies firmly. "I need Saturday and Sunday off. That was our deal."

"I'm changing the deal." My chin tilts up, and I give her a cold smile. "I've paid you a lot of money already, and I'm quite confident you're making more than you ever have before for far less hours. Are you really going to give that up?"

I expect her to drop her gaze, hunch her shoulders, and submit to me. Instead, she raises her chin higher than mine. "Yes. I'll regretfully have to give it up. I can't be available to you on the weekends. It's just not possible, so if you have to fire me for it, I understand."

"For fuck's sake," I growl as I push up from my chair to press clenched fists into my desktop. She's thwarting my efforts at taking back control. "What could be so goddamn important you'd give up this type of money for so little effort on your part?"

Hannah's golden-brown eyes darken as if they're filled with malevolent shadows. As she leans across my desk to get in my face, she snarls right back at me as. "I think my effort at my job is stupendous—or at least the way you call my name out when you come seems to indicate it is. But your money will never be as important as my freedom on the weekends."

The gritty determination in her tone gives me pause, making me curious. "What exactly is so important about your weekends?"

"I spend them with my daughter."

I jerk back, stunned by this revelation. "Daughter?"

She ignores my request for a clarification. Instead,

she coldly says, "I busted my ass at three jobs so I could make enough money to hire an attorney to fight for custody of my daughter. So while the money you pay me to do this is incredibly important, I'll go back to working three jobs before I'll give up my weekends with my kid."

Well, shit. That knocks the wind out of my sails. I'd never ask her to give that up. I might be a douche a lot of the time, but I do still have a moral compass.

"Why don't you have custody?" I ask. Well, more like demand.

Hannah grimaces. "Because the judge was a golfing buddy of my ex-husband's, and I didn't have the means to hire a very good attorney to represent me when we split."

Rage hits me again, except this time it's all for Hannah's ex. I feel an overwhelming desire to hunt this man down and beat the shit out of him.

The judge, too.

Pushing those insanely inappropriate protective feelings aside, I stand once again and grab my phone from the desk. "You can add my office to your regular schedule of cleaning. I'm going to work the rest of the day at my office."

No sense in keeping her out of here. She's seen Michelle's picture, which was really the only private thing in this space.

I don't feel the need to let her know I'm capitulating on the weekend demands, feeling she's smart enough to understand that since I just opened my personal office up to her cleaning schedule.

As I walk past her to exit, she asks, "Do you need me at the club tonight?"

Fuck, I need her right now, but I shake my head, determined to put some distance back between us. Giving into my needs means giving up control. "Not tonight. Maybe tomorrow."

Yes, I need distance. It will help me get over the fact I feel like a fool for demanding time with her this weekend, just so I could win a battle with her. I feel like a fucking fool, of course, because she won that battle fair and square.

# CHAPTER 12

## *Hannah*

NOTHING CAN STOP my hand from shaking as I unlock the door to Asher's apartment this morning. It's not because I'm still unsure of my job standing, especially after our showdown yesterday. I stood my ground on the need for free weekends, and he respected it after I explained it was because of my daughter.

Thus, I am confident I still have a job.

The reason I'm shaking is because I wonder what type of job I now have. It's clear he still wants me to clean for him, but I have no clue if he still wants *me*.

Why this is bothering me is slightly perplexing, and I've tried to break it down into something cognizable.

Asher did not want me last night. He knew he could have me at his whim and leisure, yet he declined. It could be that he doesn't want me like that anymore, but perhaps still feels bound to keep me on the payroll. In fact, it even makes sense he didn't want me at the club with him last night because he intended to avail himself of the multitude of women there who would drop to their knees for him. I've seen them before, and I've tried to ignore their hateful glares that I was with him and they were not.

The part that's causing me a whole lot of grief and uncertainty is that I seem to be feeling a little unwanted. While I don't have any aspirations of having Asher's affections, I think I've gotten way too used to having his physical attentions. In just a brief period, he has me looking at sex in a completely different way.

Hell, he has me wanting sex like I've never wanted it before.

I'm slightly ashamed that I've come to like this part of my job so much, since I still have a slight disgust in myself that I might as well be a paid whore, but I push that aside. In the end, whether I enjoy what Asher does to me or not, he is paying me very well and that will help me get Hope back.

I guess that's all that matters, so I need to be grateful for this opportunity and leave the sex out of it.

The apartment is quiet like it normally is, and I'm slightly disappointed Asher's not coming out of his office to surprise me. With a sigh, I close the door and put down the pot I'd carried in on the marble stand in the foyer. It's blue ceramic and holds yellow mums.

It's a pathetic attempt to replace the Chihuly, which was done in blues and golds. While there's obvious disparity in the value of the two items, I think his apartment is sad in its stark colors of black and white. The Chihuly was the only real color around, and I wonder why he bought it. It's so out of character with his monochromatic tastes.

I put my purse and keys on the foyer table before heading into the kitchen. It takes me all of ten minutes to wipe down the already-pristine granite countertops and wash Asher's morning coffee cup. I grab the dust rag and polish, heading back to the master suite.

Just as I'm crossing the threshold, Asher strolls out of the master bath with a thick white towel around his hips and his glossy black hair wet from the shower. Add in his contoured muscles and honey-gold skin, and it's all I can do not to sigh in satisfaction.

Ignoring the slight watering in my mouth, I exclaim, "Oh, God… I'm sorry. I didn't know you were still here."

I even avert my eyes; otherwise, I'd be overtly ogling his half-naked body.

Asher chuckles with dark amusement. Before I can react, his wet towel is smacking me in the chest.

I grab at it, my head popping up. He's grinning, totally relaxed in his nudity.

"Why so shy, Hannah?" His voice is sexy. Taunting, even. "You've seen me naked before."

I can't help myself. Taking that as tacit permission, I let my gaze run all over his well-built physique. I even stare at his cock, which is impressive in length and girth even when at rest.

When I slowly make my way back up, I find his eyes on me with an intensity that makes my legs go weak. The air between us seems to crackle, and the hair on my arms stands on ends.

"Take your clothes off," he orders gruffly.

My gaze drops back down, and I see his cock lengthening. A cramp clutches my pussy, and I don't hesitate.

I obey him at once. He smiles with dark satisfaction as I pull my t-shirt up over my head, tossing it carelessly to the ground.

My bra is barely off and falling from my fingertips before he's taking long strides across the room. He falls to his knees before me, then jerks at the button on my jeans. His movements are harsh, his breathing erratic. He gets the zipper down, roughly pulling at the denim until it's past my hips.

Asher pushes his face into my crotch, his breath hot through the cotton of my plain white panties. I feel like I could come from just the heat of his mouth. He tongues at me through the material and it joins the wetness that soaked the material when I first gazed on his naked body.

"This isn't part of our deal," I manage to gasp even as my fingers slide into his hair and grip hard to hold him to me.

He chuckles, the vibration hitting my clit before he looks up at me. "It's not against our deal either."

"True," I gasp as he stands up, lifting me easily in his arms.

The room spins, and he drops me to the mattress. More rough grabs and pulls as he disrobes me, starting with socks and shoes and ending up with my panties tossed over his shoulder to the floor.

Then his hands are in my armpits and he's lifting me, throwing me higher up the bed. He follows, crawls like a sleek cat right up my body, his eyes locked onto mine the entire time.

As his mouth comes down onto mine, his hand goes in between my legs. I'm slightly embarrassed at how easy his fingers slide into me.

"Asher," I murmur against his tongue.

When he lifts his head, I get a feral flash of teeth. "I like my name on your lips. Always so needy sounding."

His fingers are gone, but I don't feel the loss because he's sliding his thick cock into me. God, it feels so damn good. Like nothing I've ever felt before.

Is it bad I don't want to feel anything but this ever again?

Asher kisses me again and starts to move, producing groans of pleasure from us.

We've never had sex on a mattress before, and the intimacy of being in his bedroom has a profound affect. My body quickens in a way I've not felt before, and he's barely a few thrusts in before an orgasm starts to tremble.

Does Asher feel it, too? Can he feel me starting to

tighten, or maybe it's the way my fingers are digging into his shoulders?

He feels something because he starts to fuck me harder. He stops kissing me only to hover over my face, once again locking his eyes to mine.

Jaw tight, lower lip pressed between straight teeth, he fucks me with the expression on his face as well as his cock. He's totally consumed by me. Knows that fans my fire.

I explode unexpectedly, crying out as my back arches.

"Yes," he says in triumph, starting to pound even harder. Holding tight, I wrap my quavering legs around him and lock them at the ankles. I let him ride me hard. Every thrust extends my orgasm, until he goes deep, then still, and suddenly starts to unload inside of me. He shudders hard, lets out a deep groan of release, and rocks against me a few times until he collapses.

I get a short squeeze of his arms around me before he's pulling out and rolling off the bed. I gasp when he grabs an ankle, then pulls me across the mattress until I'm forced to stand beside him. He retrieves my panties and kneels before me, using the tip of his finger to slide through the semen starting to run down the inside of one thigh. I watch in fascination when his lips curl upward in satisfaction as he helps me step into my panties.

Asher slides them gently up my legs, standing along the way and arranging them into place at my hipbones.

He then cups between my legs, pressing the heel of

his hand into the wet warmth there.

Tilting his head, he whispers in my ear, "Don't you dare clean this up. I want your panties wet with me while you're working. Want you thinking about this all day."

My breath rushes out in an audible *whoosh*. I want to flop back down on the bed. Want to ask him to fuck me again.

Asher grins, winks, and then turns toward his closet. He casually tosses over his shoulder, "I'll pick you up at ten tonight."

A jolt of excitement courses through me that he's going to take me back to The Wicked Horse.

It reveals something very primal about me that I'd been suspecting but was too afraid to admit.

I crave going to that sex club very much, and I'm done apologizing for it.

While Asher dresses, I scramble into my clothes and hasten back out to the living room. I decide to start my dusting there as I've found that some distance between me and his magnetism helps just a fraction.

I've moved into the dining room, which is just an open area off the kitchen. I'm cleaning the glass table when Asher walks through. He glances at me but doesn't say a word, silently making his way to the foyer.

I watch him from the corner of my eye. When he sees the mums sitting on the pedestal, he comes to an abrupt stop. I hastily drop my attention to the glass table, pretending complete absorption in my work, but I can feel his stare on me heavy and almost accusing.

I expect him to say something. Anything. He could just as well thank me as rail at me for buying him something.

He says nothing, though. It's only when I hear the door open and close again that I relax a little. Bringing my gaze back to the mums, which are completely undisturbed, I wonder what is going through his head right now.

Does he appreciate my efforts, or does he think I'm an idiot? Perhaps they piss him off, a reminder of the expensive piece of art I so clumsily broke.

Regardless, I like them, and I can't stop the smile that spreads over my face. The flowers definitely help to brighten up the place a bit.

# CHAPTER 13

## *Asher*

THINGS HAVE CHANGED, and I have to roll with it. The downside to me fucking Hannah in my bed on Tuesday is that now I've given myself license to fuck her whenever I want. Or is that an upside?

At any rate, I'm lucky that whenever I want seems to coincide nicely with her wants. At least, she hasn't yet told me 'no' the way I've given her permission to do so.

All this week, I've been waiting for her when she walks in my apartment. I strike before she barely gets the door closed. We've christened various rooms and pieces of furniture with all kinds of dirty deeds.

I've never fucked a woman in this apartment before. Never brought one here at all, because I don't do romantic dinners or movie nights. After Michelle died, The Wicked Horse was where I went to get my kicks. What threatens to fuck with my head if I think about it too much is the fact I let Hannah into my space in a personal way, and I did it without any thought. On

Tuesday, I saw her in my room and pounced.

No thought at all.

But once that deed was done, I figured it was okay to fuck Hannah in my apartment because she's still just an employee. It's at my whim, not hers, and I don't have to stick around after to cuddle or talk about life. I went to work after, feeling fucking fantastic. Completely energized.

I've been in a good mood, or so my assistant has bluntly told me over the last few days. She actually said, "Whatever you're eating for breakfast these mornings, keep it up."

Well, these days, that would be Hannah, and her pussy definitely puts me in a great mood.

When I hear the slide of the key in the deadbolt, my body tightens. Lust courses through me. There's also an eagerness to hear her voice, which I find strange.

The door opens, and Hannah steps over the threshold. I force myself to stand my ground. Her gaze comes straight to me, a knowing smile on her face.

A ready smile.

I can't wait a moment more, so I take long strides across the living room to reach her. Cupping her face in my hands, I back her into the door. Her eyes are hot, her fingers coming up to latch around my wrists.

"Morning," she says, her voice husky and needy. It causes my dick to turn to concrete.

"Morning," I mutter before I slam my entire body

into her, knocking her against the door. My mouth descends on hers, and I don't remember kissing being this damn good with anyone else.

I consider the door I have her trapped against. We haven't had sex here. It's no Wicked Horse, but it's wild and spontaneous. I've learned I don't need the club to enjoy Hannah. In fact, the club itself doesn't do much to increase my pleasure when I'm with her. It's been consistently the same since we did away with condoms.

When I fill her up, a strange sense that I've been filled up as well takes hold of me. It's a feeling that is foreign and unique—one that applies only when I'm with Hannah. If there's one thing that concerns me about this arrangement, it's that I have to admit she makes me feel something different.

I pull my mouth from hers, intent on her clarifying one thing that I wonder about sometimes. "Tell me you want this?"

She nods, uses her hands on my head to try to pull me back into a kiss.

I use my hands on her face to hold her in place, denying her advance. "Tell me no, Hannah. Just once."

Her smile is amused. "But I only want to say yes."

"Thank fuck," I mutter before kissing her again.

Just as I start to contemplate the best way to get her clothes off—her standard uniform of a t-shirt and jeans—I'm startled by a knock on the door that we are currently pressed against.

"Just great," I growl, gently pulling Hannah away from the door. When I turn her to the side, she scrambles for the kitchen, immediately putting distance between us.

I open the door, blinking in surprise at my sister. She merely smirks at me and drawls, "Good morning."

Opening the door wider, I mutely gesture her inside. She eyes me critically, concentrating on my face for a long moment. Then her gaze brushes past me to the kitchen, her eyes going saucer wide when she sees Hannah there. Her appraisal is deliberate before she turns back to me, eyebrow raised.

"I would apologize for barging in like this, but you clearly forgot I was coming over this morning," she tells me. "At least, I think that's what your blank expression means."

There's a moment of blinking at my sister as my brain tries to process, but the only thought in my head is that I was moments away from falling into bliss with Hannah.

"My floors," Christina prompts. "I told you I was having the floors in my house redone today—that I took the day off from work to get the workers started, but that I wanted to come over here to avoid all the noise and chaos so I could at least get what work I could done. You do remember that, right?"

And yes, it all comes back to me, but it just goes to show the strength of the Hannah-haze that is left behind after just a few moments of kissing. Christ, the woman has some witchy magic.

"Yeah, I remember." I try to a smile, but because my morning with Hannah just took a solid U-turn, I say, "I'm headed into work if you want to use my office."

"Perfect." Christina beams, hitching a satchel I hadn't noticed until now higher on her shoulder. I assume she's carrying school stuff—perhaps papers to grade.

Then my sister does what my sister does best—she decides to get nosy. Without a word, she heads toward the kitchen. I have no choice but to follow.

"And who do we have here?" she asks, shooting an electrically beautiful smile of welcome and curiosity at Hannah, who returns her stare but not such a wide smile. In fact, she looks like a doe caught in the headlights.

I make hasty introductions. "This is my housekeeper, Hannah Madigan. Hannah… this is my sister, Christina."

I get an arched eyebrow from Christina, clearly showing me she's not buying this, but then she turns back to Hannah. She extends her hand. "It's nice to meet you. I can't say that Asher has ever hired someone so beautiful before, but then again, he's never hired someone solely to clean his house."

Hannah has no clue what to say. I supply the relevant info that my sister needs to hear. "I misspoke. She's more than a housekeeper. She sort of manages my household. Things like grocery shopping, handling my dry cleaning, cooking, and running errands for me."

"Hmmm," is all Christina says, not even glancing at me. She gives another warm smile to Hannah, who has yet to say a word. "Well, let's hope you keep him straight. He needs it."

To my surprise, Hannah's eyes twinkle with something I can't quite identify, but it doesn't put me at ease. She leans in closer to Christina, inclines her head in a manner I would describe as conspiratorial, and says, "Well, if I could ever teach him to put his dirty clothes in the actual hamper when he discards them, I would consider that a major victory."

My sister snorts. It's obvious to me that she's gone from being curious about this woman in my apartment to downright enraptured with her.

Grabbing Christina's arm, I give it a tug. "Let's not take up all of Hannah's time. She has a lot to do. I have to get some stuff from my office so let's go get you set up in there."

My sister doesn't hesitate. When we leave the kitchen, I shoot a look at Hannah. I'm rewarded with perhaps the best thing she could have given me this morning.

Strike that… the second-best thing.

She gives me a look of fond regret for what we were about to do and have now lost for the day. I send the same back to her, and she turns for the dishwasher.

In my office, Christina settles into the chair behind

my desk. As she unloads papers from her satchel, I load my briefcase up. It includes blueprints of a proposed wellness center that we're considering putting into one of the retirement communities we're hoping to build.

"So who is that woman really?" Christina asks in a voice that sounds casually disinterested, but she's not fooling me. She's totally nosy.

"Housekeeper," I mutter, closing my case and securing the dual latches.

"Quit fucking lying to me," she says with a laugh. "You can't hide shit from me."

"Just a housekeeper," I assert firmly as I pick my briefcase up.

"Oh yeah, then why was there a thump against the door just as I arrived? Why is your hair all mussed up? Why were her lips swollen and her cheeks flushed? I don't even want to ever think again about the hard-on I saw you sporting. And why did the two of you share a long, regretful look before we came back to your office?"

Goddamned motherfucking intuitively nosy-assed sister. She grins at me knowingly.

I deflate, sigh, and then admit a few partial truths. "She is my housekeeper. But we're sort of… seeing each other."

Delight washes over Christina's face. "Perfect. You can bring her to the gala—"

I hold my hand up, stopping her midsentence. "We're fucking each other. And that is all."

I've never held back from my sister. She's my twin after all. She can also have as foul a mouth as me, so she's not offended by my words. Christina's face crumples, and frustration washes over her. "What is wrong with you? She could sue you for sexual harassment or something."

Shaking my head, I try to ease her mind without revealing exactly how I came to have sole possession of Hannah's pussy. "It's not like that. She's a very willing participant."

"So it could turn into something more," Christina says, a happy smile pulling the corners of her mouth up once again. Not a question to me but a statement. She believes that any woman I let in can give me something she thinks I need.

I hate hurting my sister. I really do. She loves me and only wants what's best for me, but… "Sorry, it's just sex, Christina. All it will ever be."

"But—"

"No buts. Just let it go, Sis. Stop trying to push me to something you think I need, but that I clearly don't want."

A sense of capitulation is clear when she sighs and slinks back into her chair, finally giving me an acquiescent nod. I round the desk, bend over, and kiss the top of her head. "I love you. You're a pain in my ass, but at the end of the day, I still love you."

"Love you, too, you closeminded asshole," she mutters, patting my face before I pull back.

When I have my briefcase in hand and make it to my door, she asks, "Want to go out to dinner with Jack and me tonight?"

I twist my neck, glancing at her over my shoulder. "Sure. But make it no later than eight. I have plans later this evening."

"With Hannah?" she asks.

"With none of your business," I reply with a wink before leaving the office. I pull the door closed behind me, not wanting any conversation I'm getting ready to have with Hannah to carry.

I find her in the living room, cleaning my glass-top coffee table. She straightens when she hears me come in, holding a spray bottle with blue cleaner in one hand and a rag in the other.

"That was awkward," she whispers, sounding bemused.

Stepping right into her, I put a hand at the back of her head and place a long kiss on her mouth. "That was bad timing, and I'm not in a happy mood going into the office this morning."

"Poor baby," she croons, but it's sarcastic—not empathetic. "Shall we hit the club tonight?"

"Fuck yes," I reply, and then I kiss her again. "I'll pick you up at ten. And just so you know, it's going to be a long night since I won't have you on the weekend."

"Until then," she says before squatting back down to

continue cleaning my coffee table.

I watch her a moment, battling a weird feeling as she cleans. I find myself not liking it. As if the work is beneath someone like her, but then I realize… this job is a few steps above the work she was doing at that bar. I'm also paying her far more than she was making before, so I let that assuage these unusual misgivings.

Without another word or look back at her, I walk out of the apartment and head to work.

# CHAPTER 14

# *Hannah*

L EANING BACK IN the passenger seat of Asher's vehicle, I put my palms on the seat beside my thighs and rub them on the buttery-soft leather. It's decadent, which is a little how I feel right now.

After a few hours at The Wicked Horse with Asher, where he spent most of the time "playing" with me—his words, not mine—I feel akin to a goddess who has just been worshiped. I've decided to stop feeling guilty about something that makes me feel so good, which has in turn provided me with an amazing opportunity to get Hope back.

Resting my head against the seat, I smile and watch as the city lights pass us. Asher has taken to picking me up at my house on our evenings out, and then he drives me back again. He never gets out of the car, but stays parked along the curb, watching until I enter and close the door behind me. I can't figure out if he's being a gentleman or protecting his property, but either way, it's appreciated. My neighborhood can be sketchy, a mixture of older lifelong residents who want peace and quiet and a rough crowd that likes to roam the streets looking for trouble. When I was working three jobs, I was hardly ever home, so it didn't matter much to me except for that mad dash from my car to my house where I'd be relatively safe.

I always made sure Hope and I were locked inside by the time the sun set, protected by an early splurge of money after I'd moved in.

A shotgun.

My grandpa Brantley, who was my mom's father, was a good old South Carolina redneck. He taught me to hunt when I was eight, a practice I now abhor because I can't stand the thought of killing an animal. But I fondly remember the times I spent with him before he died. He was uneducated, having dropped out of high school in the tenth grade where he went on to work in a tire plant for thirty long years.

As backwoods as he was in many things, he always told me to be independent and to think for myself. He never considered me subpar because I was a woman, and he would brag to anyone who would listen that I would get a college degree one day.

That's still on my agenda despite the fact I'm twenty-seven years old, so I haven't fully let him down yet. Once I can get Hope back and get stabilized, I'll figure out my education.

Until then, I make sure to follow his biggest piece of advice to me. He had said, "Hannah Banana… if you ever need to protect yourself with a gun, do not rely on a handgun. There's too much room for error. Have a shotgun within easy reach if someone is coming at you. Just point it in their general direction, pull the trigger, and you got 'em."

"Thinking some deep thoughts." Asher's voice rolls over me like a velvety blanket.

I roll my head left and look at him. He gives me a brief glance before returning his attention back on the road. Not bothering to answer, I give him a slight shrug as I stare out the windshield, because I really don't think he wants to know anything about me. While Asher is incredibly enamored with my body, he doesn't appear to be interested in anything else about me.

Still, I'm happy with the situation.

It's the sex, of course. It makes me happy, which is perplexing because Asher is nothing to me and I'm nothing to him.

Not really.

I was in love with my husband, make no doubt about it. Really in love, and I thought sex with him was the way things were supposed to be, even the part where I had to help myself along to orgasm. But it was the love that made it good for me. The marriage of souls is special. The connection and intimacy set it apart.

Right?

Well, I don't have that with Asher. Yet, sex with him has shattered every one of my preconceived notions about sex and intimacy and how it's entwined. It makes me wonder if I even know myself at all. The things I've done with him—am willing to do with him—still astound me. I've learned and accepted a level of freedom that has enhanced my sexuality and made me feel pleasure I never knew was possible.

I can be in that club with Asher, fucking him in front of dozens of people, and like it.

A lot.

Sometimes, that makes me feel dirty, but it mostly makes me feel empowered. That is something I never felt with Nelson.

When I feel Asher's gaze on me, I ignore it. His words, though, jolt me to attention. "What's your daughter's name?"

Asher has never shown an interest in my personal life outside of manipulating things that would make me more convenient to him.

"Hope," I answer cautiously, my head now turning so I can scrutinize him. "She's five years old."

"And is her last name the same as yours?"

I nod. "Madigan was my married name. I kept it in the divorce so Hope and I would have the same last name."

His attention is solidly on the road where it should be, but he's apparently intent on conversing. "You told me you don't have custody because your husband was friends with the judge or something like that?"

The question is without an ounce of censure or condemnation in my shortcomings, but he sounds genuinely curious. I tell him the truth of it, trying to keep the bitterness in my voice to a minimum. "That's the gist of it. I mean, he was the moneymaker in the family and I was a stay-at-home mom. I didn't have much money to hire an attorney, not one who would have probably been able to get the judge moved off the case for bias or something. Apparently, the judge felt Hope would be better off with her father, who had a gorgeous mansion and a solid income, while I only have a twelfth-grade education and no real work experience."

"That's hardly fair," he says.

"Understatement of the year," I reply with a mirthless laugh. "But I did retain an attorney with the bonus you gave me, and he'll file something with the court next month."

"Why next month?"

"Because he says I need an established work history while making this nice salary you're paying me as your housekeeper. He says thirty days should do it, or actually... he said sixty would be better, but I'm impatient."

Asher is silent, and I figure he's reached his quota of curiosity about his "employee". My gaze goes back out to the street, and I realize he's in my neighborhood.

"I have a good attorney if you need help. I have my own "ins" with lots of judges if you want me to do something."

It takes effort not to gape at his generosity, but I manage a grateful smile. "I appreciate it, but I think the attorney I hired has it covered. I might need a statement from you saying I'm in your employ and that I'm an excellent worker."

Asher grins, intent on lightening the mood. "That you are. In fact, I could tell the court what a hot fuck you are. How everyone in the club wants a taste of you, but how I'd kill any one of them if they so much as touched you."

Laughing, I hitch myself up in the seat, seeing my house come into view. "You sound awful proprietary, Mr. Knight."

"I take care of my possessions," he replies smoothly, both a compliment and a putdown at the same time. He tries to lessen the sting by adding, "I treasure them."

"Like your Chihuly?" I ask with a great deal of snark as he brings his car to a stop at the curb, putting it in park. "You got over that pretty fast."

Something flashes across his face, a few emotions that are easy to read. Anger. Denial. Something else I can't quite put my finger on. His words are not surprising. "I would get over you just as fast."

I don't expect the sharp stab of pain that hits me in the chest, but I've heard far worse from Nelson. Next time, I'll be ready for his careless words and they'll do nothing more than bounce off me, but just so he knows my backbone is strong, I tell him, "Good. We're on the same page because I'd get over you easily, too. The money I'd surely miss, though."

Asher's jaw tightens, his eyes narrowing. "Then we're agreed. This is nothing more than sex. Something that could be gotten anywhere."

"Exactly," I say, reaching for the handle to open the door. I swing my legs out, pull myself into a standing position, and slam the door shut.

I turn to step onto the curb, but yelp with surprise when I see Asher standing there. His expression is bland, no trace of anger. Instead, he takes me by the hand and leads me up the little sidewalk. "I'll walk you to the door."

There's no controlling the forces of gravity, and my jaw drops open. I try to pull my hand away. "There's no need."

Asher's grip tightens, but he doesn't try to argue with me. Why should he when he's stronger and I couldn't pull my hand away now if I wanted to?

When we reach the top of the porch, Asher pulls open the screen door while I fish for my keys in my little black clutch purse. I give him my back while I unlock the door, but I can feel almost every inch of him right behind me. I can guarantee you the man isn't angling for a goodnight kiss because this isn't really a date, and besides… I sucked his cock earlier tonight. What more does he need?

When I push the door open, getting ready to offer a "goodnight" over my shoulder, I'm shocked to feel him walking in behind me.

I spin on him. "What are you doing?"

Asher gives me a wicked smile and shuts my door, casually turning the deadbolt. "Staying the night."

"I didn't invite you," I reply, and then taunt a little. "You said I wore you out at the club tonight."

"You did." He smiles slyly before stalking through my living room. I follow him down my hallway until he looks into the room he decides is mine—which is because the other has just a twin bed for Hope—and walks in there. He turns to face me. "But I'll be recharged come morning, and I'm bound and determined to have you on a weekend."

My eyes widen as understanding dawns. "You want to sleep here tonight, just because I told you I get weekends off, and you want to prove you're really in charge by fucking me on a Saturday morning?"

"I'll be satisfied with a blow job." When he grins at me, I strangely don't want to slap it off his face.

Oddly, I want him to stay the night. I wouldn't mind starting my morning off with a little bit of Asher.

"I get up early," I warn. "I like to be out of here by seven to go pick up Hope."

Asher pulls his phone out, then starts tapping on the

screen. Raising his head, he says, "I just set the alarm for six."

Jesus, I'm going to be tired tomorrow. It's just after one now, and I'm not even sure I can fall asleep with Asher in bed beside me.

But I can't say no to him, either. "Fine," I say blandly as I move past him to my dresser. I pull out a pair of pajamas—a cute short and t-shirt set—and slide the drawer shut. "But if you're a snorer, you have to move out to the couch."

Laughing, Asher lunges toward me. He snatches the pajamas out of my hands, tossing them to the floor. "Get naked. I want to feel your skin against mine tonight. Plus, it'll be easy access in the morning."

There's a womanly part of me that responds to the intimacy of those words, as noted by a strange thudding in my chest. I hold onto it as I watch Asher start to get undressed, and then I follow along.

After I turn out the lights, we slip into bed. We face each other, lying on our sides. In a million years, I would never expect him to pull me into his arms to sleep, and he doesn't. He just smiles at me in the moonlight before murmuring, "Goodnight, Hannah."

"Goodnight," I reply and close my eyes.

Despite my misgivings, I fall right asleep.

## CHAPTER 15

# Asher

A S I DRIVE to my father's house the next Saturday night, I wonder what Hannah is doing. This morning was the second week in a row that I woke up in her bed.

I did the same thing I did last week and fucked her. Rolled her onto her stomach, spread her legs, and took her from behind. Christ, I came so hard I almost passed out. Just as good as every time before… if not better.

But when I left this morning, there was one dramatic difference.

I'd felt compelled to kiss her goodbye, and I did so without any thought. She'd looked surprised.

I felt surprised.

All day, I brooded about why I would so thoughtlessly do something that showed fondness for Hannah, and then I wondered about why I cared enough to brood about it.

So I hit the gym and lifted. Afterward, I ran five

miles, thinking about Hannah the whole time. She'd said she didn't have any set plans for the day. With a goofy smile of excitement on her face, she told me she liked to do whatever Hope wanted to before she pushed me out of bed to leave. At mile four, I found myself wondering if Hannah would think of me today. By the time I finished, I'd concluded I was turning into a girl.

It was my father's phone call, insisting both his children have dinner at his house, that finally drove the consuming thoughts of Hannah far from my mind.

Sure, my dad and I occasionally meet in town for dinner and drinks, but I can't remember the last time I'd been to his house for such an occasion. Certainly not since my mother died three years ago. She'd suffered a heart attack at age sixty that had killed her quickly.

It was horrible losing her. The pain I felt was so intense, and I'd realized it was the first time I'd felt much of anything since Michelle died. It took losing my mother to realize how much I'd inadvertently disconnected from life, from my family.

I can't say enough good things about the way Christina and our mom supported me after Michelle's death. Even though I know it killed them, they did so at arm's length, somehow understanding I needed supportive space more than anything else. I got encouraging and loving phone calls and texts. We'd meet for lunch sometimes, and the talk would always be light and inconsequential.

SAWYER BENNETT

Both understood my need not to discuss Michelle and the million potential reasons she decided to kill herself.

I think they both knew I had conversations with myself daily trying to figure it out. So they watched me carefully, ready to run in should I ever decide to fall apart.

I never did.

My father, of course, was a nonentity during the times I lost the two most important women in my life, but his support was never expected. He wasn't that type of person.

The other thing my mom's passing did was to re-mind me how precious my twin was. I had disconnected from her as well when Michelle died, and losing my mom shook me up.

While I knew I couldn't open myself up to romantic love again, Christina's heart was half my own. I'd needed to accept that in my life.

These past few years, we've grown closer than ever.

Which is why I'm on edge tonight. My dad will find some way to demean Christina, and I'm going to be poised to swoop in and defend her.

I arrive at Dad's gated community. The guard doesn't recognize me because I don't come over this way much anymore. He wasn't here when my mom was alive, but that means he could have worked here anywhere from three years to three days, and I wouldn't know.

After I give my name, he checks his list, after which he opens the gate for me.

When I pull into Dad's large circular driveway, I see Christina has already arrived. She's waiting outside of her little Honda that probably has a hundred thousand miles on it. I'd love to buy her a new car, but she'd never accept it.

Well, that's not exactly true. She'd accept it, thank me, and then sell it to give the money to some pet project of hers.

I'm grinning at the thought of my do-gooder sister as I exit my vehicle.

Nodding toward the house, I tease, "Afraid to go in without me?"

She laughs and nods, reaching out to me for a hug. "Is it bad I feel like I'm walking into an ogre's house?"

Laughing in return, I squeeze her hard. It's funny but sad at the same time, especially since we grew up in this house. It's also telling that we never really refer to this as "our" house anymore. Rather, we both say it's our dad's. It became so when Mom died, as she was the only piece of glue that made us a family unit.

"What do you think he wants?" she asks me as we pull apart.

"No clue," I reply, taking her hand and marching up the wide stone steps to the double front door.

Our dad's butler answers, regally inviting us in before announcing, "Mr. Knight is in the study, and he wishes you to join him there for drinks."

Christina snickers, and I shoot her a chastising look. The butler is just doing as Dad expects him to do—to always give that air of superiority to all aspects of his life.

We continue to the study, its double doors already open to us.

Dad is standing near an empty fireplace hearth. As far as I know, it has never seen a fire, seeing as we live in the hot desert. Beside Dad is an incredibly gorgeous woman.

She seems to be the typical type of woman my dad has dated since our mother died. Much younger than him, probably in her late thirties or early forties, she's a big-busted blond. While I can't tell by looking at her, I'm guessing she's not very smart. He doesn't like women who know more than he does.

Our father turns to greet us, a big, warm smile on his face. He leaves the woman, rounds a couch that separates the room, and sticks a hand out to me. "Asher... so glad you could make it on short notice."

After I shake it, I watch in astonishment as he turns to Christina and gives her a hug.

A hug.

I can't ever remember seeing him do that. Christina's face is utterly shocked as she widens her eyes at me and awkwardly pats our father's back.

Pulling away, he smiles at Christina briefly before returning to the woman. Sliding next to her, he puts an arm around her waist. She smiles at us nervously.

"Asher… Christina… I want to introduce you to my fiancée, Mandy."

"Fiancée?" I ask, not able to hide the censure in my voice. And not because she's a young Barbie doll, but mainly because he was dating someone else just a few weeks ago. "Tell me you're kidding."

Mandy's smile crumbles, and my dad's expression turns cold. "That's rude, Asher."

"My apologies, but how can you marry someone you've probably known for five minutes?"

"That is none of your business," he retorts icily.

With significant effort, I tear my eyes from my dad to Mandy. I give her an apologetic smile. "I'm sorry, Mandy, but I'd really like to talk to my father alone if you don't mind."

"She doesn't have to go anywhere," my father snaps, pulling her in closer to him.

"It's okay, Carl," Mandy says. She gives him a slight pat on his chest. "You should talk to your children alone. I'll just go into the kitchen and check on dinner."

Not saying anything, my dad accepts her chaste kiss on his cheek. It's deadly quiet as we all watch her leave, pulling the study doors closed behind her.

The moment the doors shut, my dad turns to me and points a finger. It shakes slightly, which is a weakness I'm sure he'd rather I not see. "You will not ruin this for me. I've waited a long time to find love again—"

"You've found love with several different women since Mom died," I say dryly. I also happen to know he found love with other women when Mom was alive, but I don't mention that.

"Mandy's different," he snarls.

Christina moves to the couch to take a seat. She's not going to offer an opinion one way or the other, as I'm sure she doesn't care.

Rubbing my hand across my face, I sigh. I really don't care either, but I want to make sure he's protected just in case he's only thinking with his dick right now. "Fine. She's different. It's true love. But at least get a prenuptial signed."

My dad narrows his eyes at me. "Do you think I'm stupid? Of course I'll get one signed. I've already discussed it with her."

"And you'll ensure that Knight Investment Group is protected?"

His voice is pure ice, his glare menacing. "I taught you everything about our business. I built that company. Do you think I'd endanger it over a woman?"

No. I don't believe he would. He might think he's in love with Mandy—hell, maybe he is—but he loves power and money more than anything. He's always been that way.

I'm not given a chance to answer. My dad pivots to face Christina, who sits on the edge of the couch cushion, her hands clasped loosely on her lap. "And do you have anything to say about this?"

She gives him a bland smile. "I'm happy for you. I wish you a beautiful marriage together."

This takes my dad aback a bit. He's not used to having much interaction with Christina at all, and I think he expects her to be judgmental because they're not close.

He nods, coughing slightly before saying, "Well... okay then. It's settled. I'm marrying Mandy, and I'd appreciate it if you two were nice to her. I'm going to get her. If you'd like to stay for dinner, we'll meet you in the dining room."

Christina and I watch him walk out of his study, closing the doors behind him.

When we're alone, we both release pent-up breaths. She laughs awkwardly while I roll my eyes.

"Is it me, or has he just gotten really weird?" Christina asks as she stands up.

"I have to admit I never saw something like this coming," I muse aloud as we head to the doors together.

"Are we staying for dinner?" she inquires with a smirk.

"Sure," I say with a shrug. I don't have anything else to do since Hannah is with Hope. There is no desire in me to go to the club without her. "It could be entertaining."

"I wish Jack would have come to see this," she says dreamily as I open the door.

Chuckling, I gesture her ahead of me toward the

dining room. Who am I to judge what my dad is doing as long as he's legally protected in case she's just after his money?

Which I'm fairly sure she is, because my dad isn't the most engaging person.

Maybe he's just lonely and wants companionship. Of course, he can't just choose a nice elderly widow or something. He has to have a woman who looks like a porn star, but to each his own, I guess.

"This could be you one day," Christina murmurs.

"What?" I ask. Startled, I come to a stop in the hallway.

Her look is pointed, and there's no more amusement or joking about the situation our father just shared with us. Her voice is filled with concern. "You've closed yourself off to the possibility of love with another woman. I know you don't like to talk about it, but this will be you one day, Asher. You'll wake up, find yourself old and lonely, and you'll grab on to whatever affection gets thrown your way."

I want to scoff and blow her off. Want to be angry and tell her to mind her own business. I want to disregard everything she's said, but deep down, I know she's right. It's something I've probably known since I found Michelle dead in our bed. I realized then I couldn't ever open myself up to such a connection to another woman.

My mind automatically drifts to Hannah, specifically

last night. We fell asleep in the bed with space between us, just as we had the week before. But when I woke up this morning, I found I had somehow pulled her into me during the night. She was on my side of the bed, completely tangled up with me. Surprisingly, my first thought had been that I liked it.

Michelle and I were never big cuddlers, in or out of the bed. I wonder why that was. Was it me? Her? The way we were raised? Were we just too damn superficial? Something about that last question resonates with me.

Michelle was a good match on paper. We ran in the same wealthy circles. Both loved to discuss politics and world affairs. She made me laugh, and I did the same for her. The sex was good and plentiful. I was satisfied.

But I can't deny that it wasn't passion charged. Not the way it is with Hannah. Whether at the club, my apartment, or her house, I lust after her equally. Doesn't matter if I'm riding her from behind while people watch us at The Wicked Horse or if I'm slowly giving her a morning fuck after we wake up in her bed. It's all fucking better than anything that ever came before it.

Maybe it wasn't such a good idea to stay at her house.

Or have sex in my apartment.

Maybe I just need to keep my contact with her limited to The Wicked Horse, so the boundaries stay respected. I can't let myself be drawn into something that could cause me pain. Hannah, I'm fairly sure, could cause a world of hurt on me if I ever admitted to a very small truth.

I like what she makes me feel just a little too much.

# CHAPTER 16

# *Hannah*

"**W**ANT TO HAVE a drink first?" Asher inquires as we step out of the elevator into The Wicked Horse.

"Sure," I tell him, and he leads me over to the bar. After he has accepted a bourbon for himself and glass of wine for me, we head to a tall table in a quiet corner. The Social Room serves alcohol, but it doesn't supply much seating as the goal is to encourage people to mingle and get to know one another.

"So what did you and Hope end up doing this weekend?" he asks, and another jolt of surprise hits me. I hadn't thought Asher was interested in much other than my body.

"We went to the movies. Afterward, she convinced me into taking her to a pet store just to visit the animals, but then tried to talk me into getting a cat."

Asher laughs, leaning an elbow on the table. "I'm assuming you stood strong?"

"I'm allergic to them," I reply with a smirk. "It was an emphatic *no*."

"Way to hang tough, Hannah."

I give a wistful sigh. "Maybe a dog one day. If I get Hope back, I think a dog would be good for us."

"What's going on with that?" he asks, and it still seems like he's genuinely interested.

I narrow my eyes at him. "You know you don't have to do this, right?"

Asher frowns. "Do what?"

"Wine and dine me," I say. "Well, wine me anyway. You know I'm a sure bet."

He's not offended, only laughs at me. Leaning in, he murmurs, "Trust me, Hannah. I know the terms of our agreement exactly. But I feel like relaxing a bit with a drink, so how about you indulge me and answer my question?"

It seems legit, so I try to ignore the uncomfortable feeling that gathers in my chest at the thought he's interested in something other than my body. I give a frustrated sigh. "I can't get the attorney to call me back. I mean, he said he'd file the motion after thirty days of consistent employment, which would be the end of this week. I've left a few messages for him over the last few days, but he won't call me back."

"That's bullshit," Asher growls as he straightens slightly.

I shrug. "I'll call again tomorrow."

"Let me call my attorney tomorrow."

"What?" I exclaim. Taking in the solid set of his shoulders, I realize he's not joking. "No. You don't need to do that. Besides, I already paid a retainer to this guy and—"

"I'm calling my attorney tomorrow," he says, completely talking right over me. "I'll see what can be done."

"Asher…" I'm stuck between wanting to repel his help because I don't want any reasons to like him more than I already do… and dancing a jig for joy because I'm desperate to get Hope back and I'm tired of waiting.

He smiles at me, but then his gaze moves over my shoulder. I turn to see a very handsome man coming our way, his eyes locked onto Asher, who steps around the table to meet him.

They shake hands, and the man claps Asher on the shoulder. "Good to see you, man. You haven't been coming in as much."

That's interesting. We haven't been coming here together as much during the weekdays. I'd say about half the time, Asher seems to prefer me in his bed. If it's not in the morning, then he comes home from work before I leave and drags me in there. And for the last two weeks, he's taken to staying at my house so he can have his way with me on the weekend.

Both men turn my way, and the stranger doesn't look me up and down as so many others in this club have. He only sticks his hand out and says, "Jerico

Jameson."

"Jerico owns this place," Asher explains, then completes the introduction. "This is Hannah."

I straighten as I shake Jerico's hand. "It's nice to meet you."

"Nice to meet you as well," he says. With a twinkle in his eye, he adds, "I've been enjoying watching the two of you these last few weeks."

My face flames hot, even as I realize the thought of this gorgeous man watching me with Asher turns me on.

An arm comes around my waist, and Asher pulls me to him almost possessively. "She's not on the menu," he almost snarls, which makes my brow crinkle in confusion. He's acting as if he's… jealous? Mad? No way.

Jerico throws his head back, his laugh a booming echo. Shaking his head, he gives me an apologetic smile before turning back to Asher. "Not meaning any offense, because your lady *is* incredibly desirable, but my wife is the only one I'm interested in touching these days."

Gaze dropping to his hand, I see a shiny gold band on his left ring finger. I feel Asher relax, but then Jerico grins. "Doesn't mean I don't like watching, though."

"We don't mind you watching," Asher replies smoothly, releasing his hold on me. He steps casually back up to the table, then picks up his drink.

"Just wanted to say hello," Jerico says as he glances at his watch. "I have to get going, though."

He inclines his head. "It was nice to meet you, Hannah."

"Likewise," I murmur, wondering what his wife thinks about him owning this place.

Jerico points at Asher as he starts to back away. "How about you bring Hannah over for dinner one night this week?"

My head snaps Asher's way to see how he'll handle this incredibly awkward situation. We've essentially just been invited on a double date, and Asher and I aren't even dating.

"Can't this week," Asher replies without acknowledging my wide-eyed stare. "Heading to Florida tomorrow for business. Maybe next week."

My jaw drops. I don't even break my gaze from Asher when Jerico says, "I'll get up with you early next week."

I'm given an innocent smile when Asher turns to me. "What?"

My gaze drops, and I shrug. "Nothing. It's just… we're not…"

The words trail off as I realize I'm not exactly sure how to define what we are. We have sex. But it's more than that… The level of intimacy we share with each other is beyond anything I've ever known was possible.

"Hannah," Asher says softly to get my attention. "Would you rather me have declined and made it clear we're just fucking?"

"Why doesn't he just think that to begin with?" I ask

curiously. "This is a sex club after all."

Asher raises a brow, acting as if I'm the most naïve thing in the world. He sweeps his hand out to encompass everyone in the room. "Most of the people in here are in monogamous relationships, Hannah. But many of them enjoy swinging or engaging in group sex. This club and monogamy are not mutually exclusive. I haven't been seeing anyone but you for the past three or so weeks now. It's only logical Jerico would notice since I've never been with one woman for so long before."

"Oh," I say, fascinated by these revelations and more than a little warmed that he's never been exclusive with someone before. I decide to satisfy my curiosity a bit. "Does Jerico bring his wife here?"

Asher smiles, taking another sip of his bourbon before he nods. "A few times a week. She used to work here."

"That's interesting." I pick up my wine, study him over the edge as I bring it to my mouth. After I take a sip, I ask, "Do they swap partners?"

"Not that I've ever seen," Asher replies. "Jerico was telling the truth. He only has eyes for Trista. Occasionally, he'll double up on her with their close friend Kynan. That was the guy I talked to that first night I brought you here."

I practically choke on the wine I was just sipping. "Double up on her?"

"Fuck her at the same time," Asher says blandly, then

leans in to me. His voice drops an octave. "You know… two cocks in her at once. One in her pussy, one in her ass. Or maybe one in her ass and one in her mouth."

I swallow hard, wondering what that would be like.

Asher must see it in my eyes. "Do you want that?"

I quickly shake my head.

"Hannah… if you want it, I'll make it happen."

"You said I wasn't on the menu," I remind him.

For a moment, Asher seems flustered at the reminder of the words he spoke not long ago. Tipping his glass, he takes another sip. After he swallows, he says, "I have to admit I have pretty strong proprietary feelings about you. But if you want to feel two men inside you, I'll make it happen."

It's then I realize… I don't want another man inside me. The idea of it is all kinds of wicked and would make my panties wet if I were wearing any, but I don't want any man other than Asher touching me.

"No," I say firmly, tilting my chin up. "I'm quite satisfied with just you."

I get a grin in return, taking note of the relief in his eyes. He nods toward my wine and asks, "You want another?"

"Um… sure," I reply, enjoying the fact that Asher is willingly giving his time to me to have conversation.

After flagging a passing waitress and ordering another bourbon and wine, he turns to me.

"What did you do this weekend?" I ask pleasantly,

feeling that's a safe conversation to have.

He grimaces. "Met my dad's fiancée."

"You don't like her?" I ask with a curious tilt of my head.

"I don't like the fact that he's known her less than two weeks, she's thirty years younger than he is, and he might just be thinking with his dick."

"Are he and your mom divorced?"

Asher's gaze goes to his bourbon, a fond but sad smile on his face. "She died three years ago. Heart attack."

"I'm sorry," I say, reaching across the table to lay my hand on top of his. He's had a rough time losing both his wife and mother in the last few years. No wonder he's so guarded.

Asher raises his head, giving me a quiet smile as he pulls his hand back. He deftly changes the subject as the waitress returns with fresh drinks. "Are you sure I can't talk you into coming to Florida with me this week? As your employer, I could demand it."

Laughing, I shake my head at his persistence. I've already declined his offer twice when he asked last week. "I can't. You're not getting back until late Saturday, and I'm not giving up my time with Hope."

"Never hurts to ask." He takes a sip from his new drink.

I change the subject now. "Did you ever bring your wife here?"

Asher freezes, his gaze going slightly flat. "Why would you ask that?"

"Never hurts to ask," I say, throwing his same words back at him. Besides, I can't help but be curious about this man. "You're a sensual man, Asher. You don't hold back. I just assumed the woman you chose to spend your life with would be the same."

I think he might deny me, but his shoulders sag slightly as he shakes his head. "No. I didn't start coming to The Wicked Horse until after she died."

I'm not sure what that tells me about this enigmatic man, other than he must have changed.

I can't help but ask, "How did she die?"

Of all the things I'd expected a young woman might die from, I wasn't prepared for him to say, "She killed herself."

"Oh, God," I exclaim on a horrified exhale. My hand shoots back across the table to grab his. He reflexively jerks against me, but I hold tight. "I'm so sorry. I don't even know what to say."

Asher doesn't try to pull his hand back, but he does look everywhere but at me. Finally, he straightens, reaches for his drink with his free hand, and downs it.

I get a sharp tug and he's leading me away from the table, my new glass of wine left untouched.

Not holding back, I let him lead me where he wants. The conversation about his wife is clearly over, and there's a small tremor of fear that races up my spine as I feel waves of turmoil rolling off him.

He leads me straight to The Silo, through the heart of the room, and right to the glass room that's furthest from the door.

I've seen this room before. Seen what's inside.

The machine.

Asher nods toward it. "I want you on that tonight."

"I don't know." It comes out faint as I instinctually back slightly away.

He gives me a jerk, pulls me closer, and positions me in front of him so I stare into the room. It's already occupied as it's a popular destination.

There's a man and a woman in there, and the woman is on the machine. I clench my thighs together as I watch them, the woman's legs splayed wide as a mechanical dildo drills into her. The man with her just watches with lust-filled eyes, idly stroking his hard cock.

Asher steps in close to me, his own thick erection hard against my ass. Wrapping his arms around me, he dips his head to state, "I'm going to let that machine fuck you, and I'm going to make you suck my cock while it does. Do you like the sound of that?"

God help me and my traitorous body, but I'm nodding almost frantically as I press back into him, rotating my hips.

Laughing darkly, he holds me tightly as we watch what's going on inside. Before long, his hand has inched under my short dress, meeting no resistance since I'm bare beneath. I lean against him and close my eyes, knowing I'm in for a very wild ride tonight. Really, though, I can't think of anything else I'd rather be doing.

# CHAPTER 17

## *Asher*

FOR AGES, MEN have gone to great lengths to get laid. They've acted outrageously when the sex is good, buying their women extravagant gifts and whispering poetic words of love.

Me?

I apparently cut short my Friday meeting on the East Coast to fly back to Vegas to see Hannah. I'm making my way to her house straight from the airport, wondering if it's "too late" to stop by unannounced.

I don't really care, though. It's been a month since we've started this arrangement. Rather than getting bored, I'm wanting her even more. It doesn't help that I've been without her for three nights. Jacking off just hasn't cut it for me.

When I pull up to the curb in front of her house, I'm relieved to see her living room light on. It's getting close to midnight. I'd realized there was a good chance she'd be asleep by now. I have no clue whether I'd still go up to her house if it was dark, knowing damn well it would be rude, but that's not something I have to worry about. She's clearly up.

I get out of my car, lock it, and don't think about it again. I've given up being worried about my car in this neighborhood, figuring the benefits of being with Hannah far outweigh the cons of having my car vandalized.

I bound up the porch steps, pull her screen door open, and knock lightly. From inside, the sound of the TV can faintly be heard. After only a few moments, the door opens.

And Christ... she looks... just awful.

Hannah is wrapped up in a big fleece robe. Her hair is a stringy mess, there are dark circles under her eyes, and her nose is beet red. She's holding a wad of tissues in one hand, the other clutching her robe as if she's trying to leech warmth from it.

"Hey," she says, her voice sounding like a frog's croak.

"Jesus, Hannah," I say as I push inside. When she backpedals, I close the door, engaging the lock. "What's wrong with you?"

She waves the hand with the tissues as if nothing's wrong with her, then she croaks, "Oh... just a cold or something. I thought I'd be over it by now."

"You've been sick all week?" I ask as she shuffles back to the couch. There's a pillow, two blankets she must have been laying under, and entire coffee table overflowing with cold medicines.

"What's today? Friday?"

What the fuck? She doesn't know what day it is? "It's Friday night. Have you been working at my house all week while I've been gone?"

Hannah crawls back under the blankets on her couch, lying on her side to face me. She dabs at her nose with her tissues. "Of course I've been working. It's my job."

Rolling my eyes, I squat beside the couch. I touch the back of my hand to her forehead, finding it warm and clammy. "Have you been running a fever?"

"On and off," she replies as she nods to the coffee table. "Been taking Tylenol. It's been working mostly."

"I should probably take you to the doctor," I say. She looks like fucking death warmed over.

Hannah shakes her head. "I'm fine. It's just a cold. I'm sure I'll feel better by tomorrow."

"And you got your medical degree where?" I ask sarcastically.

She smirks, but I see the tiny shudder pass through her, which means she has a chill. "Unfortunately, I've been around the block a few times. My immune system isn't the greatest, so I tend to get a few bad colds a year. I probably picked it up from Hope. Kids spread all kinds of nasty germs from school."

She's probably right. I'm sure she knows her own

body better than I do.

In some respects, at least. I guarantee I know the area between her legs way better than she ever could.

I should go. She needs rest, and I'm not exactly the maternal caring type. Whenever Michelle was sick, she'd always shoo me away. I'd always been grateful to take the escape.

Still, I find myself asking, "When's the last time you ate? And are you dehydrated?"

Hannah shrugs. "I've been drinking some tea."

"Jesus," I mutter as I stand up. "Think you have anything here I can make that you could stomach? Or I can go out for something."

"I'm sure I have some soup in my pantry," she answers through what sounds like a rock quarry in the base of her throat.

"I'll be back." I pivot toward her tiny kitchen that's separated from her equally tiny living room by a counter.

"I'm sorry," she says, and I look over my shoulder at her. She tries to grin, but it comes off as a pathetic grimace. "You're not getting sex tonight."

"As if I'd fuck you looking like that," I retort with an evil smile. She laughs, or at least tries to, but it just sounds as if it hurts.

She's silent as I make my way through her kitchen. I find a can of alphabet soup in the pantry. Not bothering with a saucepan, I instead heat it up in her microwave after finding her bowls. I nab a spoon, some paper towels, and a bottle of water from her fridge, bringing them back into the living room. Eyeballing the coffee table, I find a spot to deposit the soup and glance over at Hannah.

Her eyes are closed, mouth parted slightly. I don't hesitate to lean over her, putting my hand to her shoulder for a gentle shake. "Wake up, Sleeping Beauty. You need to eat, then you can go back to sleep."

Hannah's eyes slowly open, and she seems confused for a minute. Pulling back the covers, I help her sit up on the edge of the couch before moving the coffee table a little closer to her.

"You good?" I ask as she takes the spoon in hand and hunches over the bowl.

"Yeah," she croaks, dipping the spoon into the bowl. "Thanks."

Taking a seat on a chair she has opposite the couch, I watch as she takes a hesitant sip. I can tell it's painful for her to swallow, and I'm thinking she should really let me take her to the doctor.

Hannah sort of freezes with the spoon halfway back to the bowl, looking at me curiously. "You can leave. You don't need to stay."

I should take the opportunity she's presenting me and hightail it out of here. I'm sure as shit not getting laid.

Instead, I glare at her. "Shut up and eat."

Hannah shrugs, then takes another delicate sip of

soup. I watch her in silence as she eats, not wanting to dissuade her with conversation.

She manages to eat half the bowl before pushing it away, and I nod toward the water. "Drink up."

I get an eyeroll, but she uncaps the bottle and takes a few sips before settling back onto the couch. She folds her legs Indian-style, pulls the blanket over her lap, and asks pointedly, "Why are you here? You should be in Florida."

My shrug is casual. "Meetings got done early so I headed back."

"I guess I should feel flattered you came by then," she says, then has a coughing fit that concerns me. I start to rise from my chair, but she waves me back down.

After another sip of water, she gives me a lukewarm smile. "I'm fine. And seriously... you should go home."

I ignore her. "If you're not better in the morning, you need to see a doctor."

I think she may argue, because she's got that stubborn little set to her jaw that turns me on when I see it. But then she just flops over on her side with a sigh of resignation as she pulls the covers over her shoulders. "Fine."

"Why don't we put you in bed?" I suggest as I stand up from the chair.

Groaning, she starts to push off the couch. "I have to change the sheets. I moved out here a few hours ago because I was sweating so badly."

I hold a hand up. "Lay back down. I'll handle it."

I have no clue where this instinct to step in and handle her comes from, but I go with it. After Hannah tells me where her sheets are, I manage to get the linens changed. Admittedly, it's been a long fucking time since I've done something like this myself. I've always had the maids do it.

When I'm done, I come back out to the living room to find her dozing. I shake her awake, then help her stand up. She's a little wobbly so I keep ahold of her as we walk down the hallway.

"I'd kill for a shower," she grumbles. "I bet I smell like a dirty sock or something."

"I'll help you take one," I offer. I'd prefer she take a bath because she can barely stand up, but her little hovel of a house only has a small standup shower. I can squeeze in with her to hold her up, and I know this because I managed to fuck her in it last week.

It takes a good half hour to manage her shower. I'm proud of myself that I didn't even get hard while standing in there with her naked. I can't say it was because she was sick and ragged looking, because truly… even on her worst day, Hannah is hot as hell. But the entire experience wasn't appealing to my sexual nature at all. Instead, I found a small measure of enjoyment in helping her wash her hair and body, while also keeping my arm around her for support.

I feel… accomplished, and it's more than surprising

to me that I like that feeling.

After her shower, she lets me dry her hair while she sits on the edge of her bed and then I dress her in a pair of her pajamas.

She's yawning heavily by the time I'm tucking her in.

"Thanks for coming by," she says quietly, then tries to level a joke my way. "I'll see you on Monday if I don't die before then."

"You're adorable. But I'm staying the night to see how you are in the morning. If you're not better, I'm taking you to the doctor."

She watches as I round the bed to climb in on the other side. I'd not bothered getting dressed again after the shower other than putting on my briefs. I'd normally take them off, but why bother? Sex isn't on the table tonight or in the morning.

When I'm settled in beside her, she reaches over and turns off her bedside light, casting the room into darkness. I can feel her shift, turning on her side to face me, which is how we go to sleep together.

"Thanks again," she says.

"No problem," I say, reaching blindly across the bed to touch her face. It's cooler, which is reassuring.

There's silence as I withdraw, so I close my eyes to go to sleep.

AWAKENING THE NEXT morning to an empty bed, I roll

off the mattress and head to the bathroom for a morning piss before finding Hannah in the kitchen.

She's sitting at the two-person table with a cup of tea in front of her, surfing her phone. There's an empty plate with breadcrumbs on it. I'm assuming it held toast.

"How do you feel?" I ask as I walk toward her. Reaching out, I touch her forehead and find it to be completely cool. Her eyes seem a little brighter this morning as well.

"Much better," she says, her voice still coarse but stronger sounding. "I'm going to pick up Hope around noon."

"That's great," I reply, moving over to her Keurig. Hannah is a coffee drinker like me, so the fact she's drinking tea tells me she's still a little shaky. But since she's cool to the touch and determined to see her daughter today—which is no surprise at all—I don't feel the need to badger her to go to the doctor.

I make a cup of coffee and take it back to the table, sitting in the chair across from her. Stretching my legs out, I brush up against hers, marveling at how good she feels just from that simple touch. I'm in no way thinking about sex with her, but fuck if just our legs touching isn't like grabbing hold of a live wire.

I take a sip of my coffee and set the cup down. "Listen… I talked to my lawyer about your situation with Hope."

"Oh," she says, her eyes widening with interest as she

leans forward, crossing her arms on the table. I can tell she completely forgot about it.

"My attorney will jump right on this. File a motion Monday morning."

"But I already have an attorney," she points out.

"One who won't return your calls," I counter. "I guarantee you that my attorney will call you back the same day if you have a question."

And I know that because he knows I'd fire his ass if he didn't.

"But I already paid a five-thousand-dollar retainer to the other attorney."

"You can get that back, Hannah."

She chews on her lower lip. It makes me want to kiss her. I wonder if she's contagious.

Her tone is still dubious. "But my attorney said I need a longer work history to show the court I'm stable."

"My attorney says not to worry about that at all," I tell her.

Which is sort of true, but sort of not true. He said work history is important, and he readily accepted it as the truth when I told him Hannah had been working for me for three months as an executive assistant.

I'm struck almost stupid when she levels a blinding smile at me, and I realize I've never seen her this genuinely excited about something before. "Okay... I'll use your attorney. And I've still got most of the bonus you gave me, which I can use to pay him."

"Don't worry about that." I wave my hand. "He's on a permanent retainer with me so he can jump on this Monday. You and I will settle later. Besides… I'd rather you take that money and move into a safer neighborhood."

"If I get Hope back," she murmurs, her gaze dropping to her cup of tea.

"You will," I say confidently. My attorney truly did feel good about this case after he'd had a chance to investigate it this week. He looked up the file at the courthouse, and he's of the belief Hannah totally got cooked by the judge because of his friendship with her ex.

"Thank you," Hannah says with a smile, bumping her leg against mine. "I hate to say it, but breaking that Chihuly vase of yours changed my life for the better."

It's a sweet sentiment, and one that wouldn't normally affect me.

But it does now, in the most uncomfortable of ways, and all I can think is that my life has changed, too.

# CHAPTER 18

S TEPPING INTO ASHER'S bedroom, I take a moment to study him as he sleeps. I never realized what a fierce expression he always kept on his face but now that he's relaxed and not aware of anyone watching him, he almost looks vulnerable.

Which is not a word I'd ever use to describe Asher Knight. And if I did, he'd take great offense to it. In the past month, I've come to understand some important truths about him.

He's bossy, arrogant, and a control freak. He's strong and determined. The vibe around him is always one of authority, and when he wants something, he takes it.

I also found out just a few days ago that he has an incredibly surprising softer side, as evidenced by the way he took care of me Friday night when I was sick. I didn't think he had something like that in him, and it absolutely goes against everything that our relationship stands for. He went one step further by helping to push my case forward to get Hope back. True to his word, his attorney is filing the motion today. It will be served upon Nelson and his attorney, and I've been tense all morning waiting for a phone call from him.

I woke up feeling so much better on Saturday morning, which was a relief, because that meant I would get my time with Hope. But I was feeling a tad guilty when I noticed that Asher had a bit of a cough as he was leaving.

"I hope you didn't get sick from me," I'd told him from the doorway as he walked down my porch.

He waved me off. "Just a tickle in my throat. I'm fine."

When I came into work this Monday morning, I found Asher in bed with a fever, sweats, and a deep congestive cough. I immediately hooked him up with some tea. Because he had no cold medications in his apartment, I ran out to the pharmacy to grab the necessities.

I dosed him up and ordered him to sleep, which is really the best sort of medicine. His body was fighting off some nasty stuff because he didn't even try to argue with me.

But now it's close to lunchtime, and he needs to eat and hydrate. I carry a tray stacked with chicken noodle soup, crackers, and some Gatorade. It's time for him to take more Tylenol, too, if he's still hot.

I set the tray on the side table and turn to the bed. I can't help but stare just a moment more because in sleep, he looks boyishly handsome. And even though he's sick, he's incredibly hot. He's kicked off all the covers, wearing only a pair of briefs that make me drool.

Touching a hand to his forehead first, I note it's cooler to the touch. He doesn't stir so I gently shake him by the shoulder. "Asher... wake up."

His eyes flutter open slowly. Dazed, he looks at me. "Hey."

"I want you to try to eat something, and you also need to also drink some Gatorade."

"Not hungry," he says with the same froggy-sounding voice I had a few days ago. Yup... fairly sure I got him sick, and it was probably because he held me through the night. It's an odd feeling but one I don't hate. While he shows me no other physical affection except when we're having sex, I can't help but think it must mean something, right?

I have no intention of coddling him through his illness. Instead, I intend for him to follow my directions to get better quicker. Due to my compromised immune system, I've unfortunately had too many of these illnesses the last few years, I know the best way to knock them out.

Grabbing his pillow, I give it a little jerk as I order him, "Sit up so I can put this tray on your lap."

"Rather have you on my lap," he croaks, but there's no power or punch in his words. This cold is whipping his butt. It's not a serious offer.

Pity. I do miss sex with him.

Thankfully, he doesn't fight me and manages to haul

himself up to lean against the headboard. I put the tray on his lap, then open the Gatorade bottle while he picks up the spoon and pokes around at some of the noodles.

"What time is it?" he asks.

Turning to his table, I start picking up discarded tissues, an empty glass that had had ginger ale in it from earlier this morning, and a box of Nyquil gel caps. "Almost noon."

"I need to get into the office," he mutters, then has a coughing fit.

"I'd advise against it."

He glances from me to his soup, dipping his spoon in before guiding it to his mouth. When he swallows, he points the spoon at me. "You're awful bossy. I think it's because you know I'm too sick to spank you."

God… he spanks so well.

"Tell you what," I suggest. "You eat your soup, drink all the Gatorade, and then promise me you'll close your eyes and lay there for fifteen minutes afterward. If you're still awake, you can go to the office. My bet is you're going to fall back asleep."

Asher nods, a small tell that he agrees with me. He gamely tries another spoonful of the soup.

I turn for the door. "Call me if you need anything."

"Thank you, Hannah," he says roughly.

I glance at him over my shoulder, smiling at the expression on his face. He hates being helpless and yeah… I do feel a bit powerful right now. "Repaying the favor," I say.

Closing the door, I head into the kitchen. My goal today is to clean all the windows in the apartment and dust the baseboards. I started coming up with projects like this to fill my time, as keeping his place clean and doing some errands for him doesn't always keep me busy. I know our sexual escapades together are considered "work time" for me, but I never want to be looked at as someone who doesn't work hard.

I'm startled when I enter the kitchen to find Asher's sister standing at the big center island. Christina is just setting down her purse and keys there, so it's obvious she just arrived.

"Hey," I say with a warm flush rushing over my face. I feel like I've been caught doing something naughty, having just left Asher mostly naked in his room, despite my noble actions of caring for him when he's sick. Probably latent guilt for having been ogling the sick man just moment ago.

"Hey," Christina says with a smile that is etched with worry. "I tried to call Asher this morning, but he didn't return my call. I called his office and they said he was home sick, so I just came by to check on him."

I throw my thumb over my shoulder toward his room. "He's in bed. I just gave him some soup and Gatorade."

"Well, that's sweet of you," she replies. "Thank goodness you were here to see to him."

"It's my job," I murmur with a small bob of my head. I move around the island, then squat in front of the sink cabinet where the glass cleaning supplies will be.

It's silent so I dare to peek up at Christina, who is now smiling down at me with what I would describe as a "knowing" look.

Oh my God. Does she know I was just ogling her almost naked brother?

My cheeks heat a little more and I open the cabinet, sticking my head inside to root around.

"I'll just pop in to see if there's anything I can do for him, but it looks like he's well-tended here."

"Uh-huh," I reply vaguely, keeping my head inside the cabinet so I don't have to converse with her.

I hear Christina move out of the kitchen, assume she's into the hallway, and I pull back with glass cleaner in one hand and paper towels in the other.

I'm not sure why I want to hide the nature of my relationship with her brother, but I never wanted to be the maid or secretary the boss banged. It seems seedy.

An unbidden laugh wells up inside of me as I realize how ludicrous it is to feel that way, given the fact I actually *am* banging him and I've been paid money to do it, too, which is far worse.

I make it no further than finishing the first full window in Asher's living room, when Christina comes back in.

Instead of going toward her purse in the kitchen,

though, she heads my way. To my horror, she plops down on the couch. She even curls her feet up under her as if she's settling in for a good long while.

"He's almost done eating," Christina informs me as I turn to spray cleaner on the next window.

"That's great," I mutter in reply, but offer no more.

"He said you ordered him to take a nap after."

"Um… yeah," I admit, using paper towels to wipe the windows down.

"No one," Christina says in a voice that's tinged with awe, "and I mean no one, orders Asher to do anything."

My entire body goes warm. I realize Christina has guessed far more about our relationship than I could have ever given her credit for.

I slowly turn around to face her, prepared to lie and deny.

When I meet her gaze, I'm stunned to see pure joy reflected at me.

"This is great," she says in a conspiratorial whisper as she leans forward on the couch.

"What's great?" I ask quietly, glancing to the hallway that leads to Asher's room, then back to his sister. Can he hear us?

I take a step closer to her just so we can keep the conversation on the down low.

"You and Asher," she says smugly.

I shake my head and hold my hands out, one still clutching paper towels. "No, no, no, no. You've got the wrong idea."

"I don't," she says with a tip of her chin upward. "You're taking care of my sick brother, who is half naked in his room, and you're ordering him around, which can only mean you have him by the short hairs. I know my brother, and he would never, ever let anyone cater to him like this."

The deer-in-the-headlights look is all I can manage in return.

"And I think it's wonderful he's let someone else in," she goes on, still whispering. This tells me she very much doesn't want her brother hearing this.

Five seconds ago, I was all lie and deny, but now I do sort of a double take on the situation. She's piqued my interest.

"Let someone else in?" I ask for clarification.

My body takes an unconscious step toward her, clearly showing my curiosity. I should just go back to work and ignore her, but really... am I going to pass up a chance to get some insight into Asher? Not if she's willing to offer it up without demanding something in return, and she seems like she's willing to dish with me.

"He's just been so closed off from everyone since Michelle died." Her voice is mournful, but I'm not sure if it's from losing Michelle or her brother in the process.

"He told me she killed herself," I murmur, feeling a heaviness in my heart for Asher.

Christina nods. "He found her. In their bed. While

he won't talk about it, I think he blames himself."

"Why would he do that?" I ask, horrified.

"Asher can do anything. Fix anything. But I think he feels like a failure for not recognizing she was in crisis."

"It's not always visible," I say. I know this because I had a friend—not close, but a friend just the same—who killed herself in high school. I'd been stunned. The day she did it, she hadn't seemed sad or depressed at all. Our school counselors talked to us candidly about suicide and depression, telling us it just isn't as transparent as people would like to think.

"I know that," she says. "And he probably does deep down, but still… I think he wanted to remove himself from any attachments going forward. He moved out of their house and into this apartment. Since then, he's not taken a single interest in developing friends or a romantic relationship."

"We don't have a romantic relationship," I feel compelled to admit.

She smiles slyly as she pushes off the couch. Stepping into me, Christina says, "You have something, and that's good enough for me right now."

Right now?

What does that mean?

I have no clue because she turns and heads to the kitchen, snagging up her purse and keys. I get a beautiful smile from her when she turns back to me. "Maybe you and I could have lunch sometime. Talk some more."

"Um… yeah," I mumble, but that thought terrifies me. I don't want to do anything to overstep my bounds. The last thing I want is Asher pissed at me.

With a wave, Christina breezes right out the door. I stand there for almost a full minute before I jolt with the realization I'm at work and have shit to do.

I return to the windows and finish the living room.

After, I head to Asher's bedroom, completely satisfied when I see him conked out. After I quietly gather the tray from the table, I leave the room. I just manage to pull the door shut with one hand while balancing the tray on the other, when my phone loudly rings from my back pocket.

I snatch it out, quickly answering the call without even seeing who it's from.

"Hello," I say quietly as I head toward the kitchen.

"Hi, Miss Madigan?" a female voice says.

"Yes?"

"This is Anne Marie calling from Dr. Yonkowski's office. It's time to schedule your bi-annual follow up with him."

There's no stopping the chill in my veins at the re-minder, despite the fact I probably have nothing to worry about. "Has it been six months already?"

"Sure has," she chirps. "You been doing all right, honey?"

"Um… yeah. Had a few colds this year—one just last week. Otherwise, I feel great."

"Your immune system is going to struggle a bit," she says, telling me something I'm already aware of. "I recommend zinc."

"Zinc. Got it."

"Okay, let me pull up the doc's schedule," she says, and I can hear her fingers tapping on a keyboard.

She offers me up some dates, the soonest of which is three weeks away. That's fine, though, as this is just a regular follow-up and there's no urgency.

She promises to send me a printed reminder letter before we hang up, but I still put it in the calendar on my phone.

*Monday, November 19, 2:00 PM*
*Las Vegas Hematology and Oncology.*

I make a mental note to myself to let Asher know I'll need off early that day, assuming he still wants me then. I fully expect there to come a day when he gets tired of this relationship, and all I can hope is that he'll keep me on cleaning his apartment until I can find something to compensate.

My thoughts then turn back to Dr. Yonkowski, the oncologist who treated me after I was diagnosed with Hodgkin's Lymphoma three years ago. It was caught so early that I was one of those lucky, lucky people who fall into the ninety-percent survival rate. So far, I've been doing great. I have to see Dr. Yonkowski twice a year now and I tend to get sicker a little easier with colds and such, but mostly, I couldn't ask for anything more.

Well, hitting the five-year mark will be a total high-five moment with myself. Maybe I'll buy myself a cupcake on that day.

There would be no one else to celebrate it with me. Hope was only two when I was diagnosed, and she never knew or understood what happened. I drove myself to all my appointments, often with Hope in tow. Nelson couldn't be bothered to attend with me because, as he'd said on so many occasions, "It's just stage 1 cancer. It's totally curable."

That wasn't exactly true but still, it was the best prognosis I could have hoped for. I downplayed everything with my mom and brothers, assuring them Nelson was being supportive. Otherwise, they would have stormed Vegas. Frankly, they just couldn't afford to.

So, I was on my own and I went through it alone. I came out on the tail end knowing I could handle anything. Being diagnosed with cancer and fighting it alone with no support taught me more about myself than I could have ever hoped for. It gave me the courage to finally walk away from Nelson, knowing I had nothing to be scared of. I'd already conquered the ultimate fear.

I'm a better person today because of it.

# CHAPTER 19

## *Asher*

I CAN'T FIGURE out the exact moment when I apparently decided Hannah was not just an employee to me, but I'm embracing it right this moment as I hunt her ex-husband down.

I need to have a come-to-Jesus meeting with him.

My week was shot to shit by getting sick. It took me a few days to get over it completely. After that first day when Hannah insisted I hydrate and sleep, I started feeling much better. I spent the rest of the week catching up on rescheduled meetings, reviewing reports and legal documents, and meeting with my attorneys on some potential bids we are considering making at a property auction.

By the time I was able to see Hannah last night at the club, between her illness and mine, as well as my business trip last week, it had been six days since I'd had her.

The sex was better than ever. I want her more today than I did last night. My interest in her isn't waning at all.

All things that concern me because it's in direct opposition to how I've decided to lead my life.

Without connections or responsibilities to another human. A plan to keep my distance and keep my heart safe.

Which makes it insane I'm here at a construction site that Nelson Madigan is supposed to be on, intending to fix some shit for Hannah.

Last night as I was taking her home, I'd asked her casually if she'd heard anything from her ex since the motion was filed. I'd asked my attorney about it. While he must observe the rules of confidentiality and can't tell me details, he told me he hadn't heard anything from Nelson's attorney.

But Hannah wasn't so lucky.

Apparently, she's been hearing quite an earful this entire week from her ex, but it isn't what I expected. I figured the guy would be pissed, maybe try to threaten and bully her into backing off. For that, I'd gladly whip his ass, but that's not what he did at all.

Instead, he systematically flooded Hannah with calls and texts that were taunting and degrading. He laughed at her notion that she'd ever be able to stand opposed to him. He pointed out her lack of funds, education, and a solid work history. The douche mocked her, daring her to go forward. He said she'd be wasting all her money and he'd win once again. Hannah didn't seem all that perturbed about his behavior, which told me he must have been quite the bully throughout their relationship. She was apparently used to it and blew it off.

I couldn't let it go though.

I'd gotten home yesterday and shot a text to my attorney, knowing it would wake him up and not caring. My request was simple.

*Tell me where Nelson Madigan will be tomorrow.*

I have no clue how he came by the information, but I had it by nine AM along with a warning. "Don't do something that will get you arrested. I have to be in court this afternoon, so I won't be able to bail you out until after that."

I assured him I had no intention of starting anything, but that would only hold true as long as Nelson Madigan spoke about his ex-wife with respect during our conversation.

If not, then... well, no telling what would happen.

As I exit my car and start heading across the site to the main office building—one of those temporary-type trailers—I take in the activity around me. I find it interesting—almost serendipitous—that Nelson Madigan works in the same industry as me.

I stake financing into large real estate ventures, while Nelson's company takes the money and builds. While I've never met him before, I do recognize his company's name. It's a pretty prominent and well-respected commercial building company, which has done work with Knight Investment Group in the past.

I've decided to use this "past history" to get all up in Hannah's business and set her ex-husband straight.

After reaching the trailer, I bound up the four wooden steps and rap sharply on the door before I open it.

Three men are standing around a drafting table, studying blueprints. Their heads pop up when I enter and close the door behind me.

Their facial expressions transform, each recognizing me and seeming shocked to find Asher Knight, the man supplying the money for some of their projects in the past and potentially in the future, standing in their tin trailer office.

"I'm looking for Nelson Madigan," I say to the group, my gaze moving back and forth among the men.

A man with slicked-back dark hair and a poor attempt at a goatee steps forward with a broad smile on his face, sticking his hand out. "That's me, Mr. Knight. It's a pleasure to meet you."

"Likewise," I say easily as we shake. Releasing him, I turn to the other two men. "Do you mind excusing us for a moment? I need to discuss something personal with Nelson."

The men nod, giving me smiles as they make their way out. Once we're alone, Nelson offers me coffee or water, but I decline.

"What can I do for you?" he asks with a level of excitement in his voice he just can't contain. My presence here could mean important things for him.

I go ahead and dangle the carrot right off the bat. "I'm sure you've heard, but we'll be closing on the Tyndall property in a few weeks."

He nods, his tongue practically hanging out of his mouth. "It's been the talk of Vegas. Everyone's wondering what you're going to do with it."

"High-end retirement community," I say blandly. "Residential and commercial opportunities."

"Well, you know my company will be bidding," he replies. "I'd love the opportunity to work with Knight Investment Group again."

"The bid is yours if you don't oppose your ex-wife's request to obtain custody of your daughter. And I'm talking full custody, not partial. You can still have visitation, of course," I add magnanimously.

Nelson's face goes blank for a moment, his jaw dropping slightly. Then it flushes red as a small vein starts to pulse in his forehead. "What has that bitch done now? Has she gone to you with some fucking sob story to get you to lobby on her behalf? Because I can tell you, you can't believe a word out of her mouth. She's batshit crazy."

"Careful now," I warn, voice low and sounding dangerous even to my own ears. I take a step closer to him. "Your ex-wife is a very valued employee of mine and I like to help my employees, especially when they're being bullied by dickless bastards like you who enjoy belittling women."

"What—that—if she—" he stammers, clearly confused over this turn of events.

"Let's face it," I say calmly. "The only reason you wanted custody of your daughter was because it would hurt your ex-wife, who hurt you by leaving after you cheated on her. It's all about your ego. I'm here to offer you a way out. I'll give your company the bid—if it's within reasonable standards—and you let Hannah have her daughter full time. You will also pay proper child support, and you'll stop being an ass to her. Move on, Nelson. It's pathetic you can't let that shit go."

Apparently, he's not offended by my words, because he hasn't heard one single bad thing I've said about him. Rather, he's stuck on me guaranteeing him the bid on the Tyndall project. It's worth millions, of course.

"You guarantee the bid to my company?" he asks suspiciously.

"As long as it's within reasonable standards," I reiterate.

The fuck spends no consideration whatsoever on whether he'd even like to keep his daughter. All he does is flash a cheesy smile and say, "Deal."

A goddamn prick is what he is.

He holds his hand out to me to shake, but I ignore it, further instructing him. "You will not tell Hannah about this. And if you ever tell your daughter you sold her out for a construction deal, I'll kill you."

Nelson's face goes beet red again, but he holds his tongue. The pull of millions of dollars just made his ego, along with his daughter, expendable.

"You call your attorney and tell him to make it happen. Being respectful to Hannah is a requirement, too. If she gets upset about anything, not only is the deal dead, but I'll also drive your company into the ground."

"Understood," he says through gritted teeth, and there's no doubt now that he's pissed.

I extend him a curt nod of farewell, turning for the door.

His next words stop me cold in my tracks. "You fucking Hannah?"

Pivoting around, I level him with a glare that makes him shrink backward.

But I don't lie to him. "That's none of your business."

He merely nods, not actually caring if I am or not. He's already spending the money he's going to make.

"Call your attorney ASAP, Nelson," I remind him again. "I want Hannah to have the good news before the end of the day."

He doesn't reply, but I don't wait for it either. I trot out of the temporary office trailer, pulling my sunglasses out of the interior breast pocket of my suit.

I just set the wheels in motion that will ensure Hannah is no longer available to me on weeknights. I have to figure out what to do with my life now. Do I accept the limited contact or cut her loose completely?

I will never be her priority, and that is truly the way it should be. Hope is what should be important, and there's a part of me that's proud of what I've done.

I put Hannah and Hope's needs above my own, and I feel good about it. I want Hannah to be happy, and let's face it… eventually, I'll probably hurt her anyway.

Yeah… this was a good thing.

I start whistling a jaunty tune as I stroll across the packed dirt site to my McLaren.

# CHAPTER 20

## *Hannah*

I PULL THE chicken parm out of the oven, setting it on top of the gas-range burners to cool. Normally when I make dinner for Asher, I prepare a single dinner portion for him and package the rest to freeze, but I don't have time to wait for it to cool down. I got behind on my day today with a late start out of my neighborhood due to a flat tire.

I tried to change it myself by watching a few YouTube videos, but luckily a passerby took pity on me as I was struggling get the jack lined up properly. Even as I gratefully accepted his help, I'd vowed I'd learn how to do it myself so I wouldn't have to be dependent on a stranger if it happened again.

Moving around the kitchen, I flip off the kitchen lights, check to make sure nothing is out of place, and then nab my purse and keys from the counter. I make it no more than halfway across the living room before Asher comes in his front door.

"What are you doing home so early?" I ask, glancing down at my watch to see it's barely six. That's early for Asher, who is a bit of a workaholic. On some nights, he never even makes it home for dinner, but rather leaves straight from work to collect me for our Wicked Horse adventures. That even includes Friday nights. I've never seen him start his weekend this early.

"Late meeting I had got cancelled so I decided to call it a day," he drawls as he casually saunters in.

He always does it, and I'm never prepared for it.

Let's his eyes roam all over me when he first sees me on any particular day, I mean. Sometimes, it's in the morning if he's still here when I arrive. Other times, he doesn't see me until he picks me up for an evening at the club.

But right now, he takes me in slowly in a way that makes my skin tingle from his attention. He never kisses me hello, but I'm not sure that would matter. Everything in the way he regards me right now is more than any girl could ever want when a man acknowledges our beauty and desirability.

His perusal stops at my face, his eyes lighting up with a low smolder. I brace myself for him to haul me off to the bedroom. Instead, he sniffs the air. "What smells so good?"

"Chicken parm," I reply, backing away from potential sexual fantasies and entering the reality of his dinner on the stove. Before I start to leave, I say, "I just pulled it out, so you should tuck in sooner rather than later. I didn't get a chance to freeze the rest. Sorry, but I was running late today."

As I'm walking past Asher, he takes my arm. The warmth of his touch affects me too much, so I swallow hard and look at him.

"Why were you late?" he asks curiously.

"Flat tire."

He doesn't say anything, but seems to be deeply thinking about something as he gazes at me. It makes me nervous, like he's plotting.

Nervousness causes me to ramble. "I've got to get going. Got errands to run. Plus, I need to eat, take a shower, and get ready before you pick me up tonight."

Asher's brows pull inward a bit, as if he's contemplating something deep and secretive that only he will ever know, but then smooths out just as quickly.

Smiling faintly, he steers me back toward the kitchen, tugging gently on my purse to take it off my shoulders. "Stay. Eat dinner with me."

Stopping dead in my tracks, I crinkle my brow at him. My skepticism must be clear on my face, because it makes him laugh.

Releasing my arm, he points toward the stove. "Dish us up two plates, Hannah. I'm starved."

"You want me to stay for dinner?" I ask hesitantly.

Asher doesn't answer right away. Instead, he takes off his suit jacket and hangs it over the back of one of the island stools. He walks to the sink, unbuttons his shirtsleeves, and rolls them up a bit so he can wash his hands.

God, he's got great forearms. Tanned, strong, with just the right amount of dark hair and tight muscles.

"Stay for dinner," he repeats, which doesn't exactly answer my question. I asked if he "wanted" me to stay, which is a whole lot different than him commanding me to stay.

I look at my watch again. "I really have to hit the grocery store. I'm all out of Hope's favorite things."

"Which are?" he asks with what I swear is genuine interest. He then makes another pointed nod at the chicken parm while he dries his hands.

With a sigh, I decide to eat with him. I can always do the grocery store tomorrow. After I dump my purse back on the counter, I pull two plates from his cabinet while I answer his question. "Let's see… Hope's favorites. She loves Gogurt, chocolate milk, Goldfish, and strawberries to name a few."

"What the hell is Gogurt?" he asks with a grimace.

Laughing, I grab a spatula to dish out the chicken breasts. "It's yogurt in a plastic tube. You don't need a spoon; you can just suck it out. Can even freeze them to make a frozen yogurt popsicle. They are surprisingly good."

A thoughtful expression passes over his face as he crosses his arms and leans a hip against the counter to watch me. "Huh," is all he finally says.

I chuckle again. "You haven't been around kids much, have you?"

"Not really. I have some acquaintances who have kids, and I see them at events or holiday parties. But honestly, my social circle isn't that diverse."

"Diverse?"

He grins. "You know… my social circle is other rich billionaire workaholics who meet up occasionally on the golf course."

"Aaah," I say with a mocking grin. "Your life is so tough."

I'm rewarded with a rich laugh from him that says it's okay for me to make fun of his money. He's not offended.

I pick up the plates and turn to set them on the island, which is where I assume we'll eat. It's casual, and I don't think I've ever seen Asher use his dining room.

And because the conversation has been easy and natural since he got home, and he appears to be in a very relaxed mood, I ask, "Did you and Michelle ever want kids?"

There's a terrible moment where everything seems to freeze. Asher's eyes go blank. I stand still, holding the two plates of chicken parm in my hands, thinking I just overstepped a very bright line of separation between employer and employee. It's a colossal mistake, and my mind races over how to fix it.

But before I can come up with anything, Asher moves to a small wine shelf he has built into the lower cabinets and pulls out a bottle of red.

He holds it up to me, silently asking if I'd like a glass. I nod in return, still standing frozen with the plates in my hands.

I'm able to finally breathe when Asher starts talking as he uncorks the wine. "We never really talked about kids that much. I was sort of focused on my career. I thought we had all the time in the world, and well... Michelle flat out said she didn't want them. I figured she would potentially change her mind one day down the road, but it just wasn't something that was important to us in our short marriage."

I put the plates in front of two stools, then grab utensils, feeling slightly guilty for admitting, "Sometimes I wish I hadn't had Hope when I was so young."

"How old were you?" he asks as he pours the wine.

"Twenty-two," I say, realizing... he now knows how old I am. He's never asked before, but he knows Hope is five so that puts me at twenty-seven. I wonder if that is even important to him, but I think not.

"Not overly young," he says with a shrug, but then I'm floored when he says, "With Michelle... I wonder if, deep down, maybe she knew she wasn't strong enough to be a mother."

A lump forms in my throat as I round the island. He comes from the opposite side, eyes full of what looks like fear for even letting me in.

"No one really knows if they're strong enough to be a mother," I say. "I know I had my doubts. Still do for that matter."

He gives me a grateful smile that I've pulled the attention away from Michelle and put it back on me. I'm moving away from such a sensitive subject because I know it makes him uncomfortable. Despite my insane curiosity to know this man on a deeper level, it's obvious he doesn't want that. He's made that clear in the past, as did his sister earlier this week.

Asher sets the glasses down before pulling a stool out for me. I take it. When he's seated beside me, we both take sips of our wine.

I set my glass down and pick up my utensils. "Speaking of kids… do you want me to grab some Halloween candy for next week?"

Asher frowns as he cuts into his chicken. "Why?

"Because I'm sure you'll get trick or treaters in your building. Don't want to get caught without any candy to hand out, do you?"

Asher gives me a sidelong, evil grin. "I intend to do what my father always did on Halloween. He turned off all the lights and hid in the basement until it was over."

"You don't have a basement," I point out dryly.

"I don't have windows on the front of my apartment for anyone to see me in here hiding, either."

Laughing, I stab my fork in the air at him. "Touché."

Asher eats a bite of chicken, groaning with delight. "This is fantastic."

"Thanks."

"You going to take Hope trick or treating?"

"Yup," I say, feeling a tiny surge of excitement. "Nelson always hated doing it, but I love it. And she wants to be a fairy princess this year. I found an amazing dress for her online. It was a little expensive, but I felt like splurging on her. I don't get to do it often."

Asher's smile is warm as he continues to cut up his chicken. "Where will you take her?"

"Just our neighborhood," I reply, carving out another piece to put in my mouth. I wish I'd made some pasta with it. I'm a pasta freak. Chicken parm without rigatoni seems like a travesty.

"The fuck you will," Asher says as he turns to face me. Setting his utensils down, he adds, "You'd probably get mugged before you made it half a block."

I roll my eyes, plopping a piece of chicken in my mouth. He just glares at me so after I swallow, I say, "It's not that bad. There are nice people in the neighborhood, and I'm sure there will be lots of people out."

Asher opens his mouth to argue, and I'm sure it would be entertaining, but my phone rings. I groan. It's the ringtone I'd set for Nelson.

"I seriously don't want to answer that," I say as I look forlornly at my purse where my phone is. But I have to because as much as I'm sure that he's calling to taunt me again, in the off chance it's about Hope or something happened to her, I always have to answer his call.

Leaning over the counter, I grab my phone from my purse. My tone is flat when I answer, "What is it, Nelson?"

He cuts right to the chase. It's something I could have never expected in my wildest dreams. "I've decided not to fight you on custody of Hope. I'm going to agree to let you have full and primary, and I'll take visitation on every other weekend. We can rotate holidays."

My entire body turns to jelly, and I sag in my seat. My heart starts thumping so hard I'm afraid it will burst out of my chest. "Are you serious?"

He's so matter of fact. So unemotional about giving up his child. "Yes. I've got a big project coming up, and it will be difficult to care for her."

He means it will be difficult to get one of his floozy women to watch her.

But I don't say that. I don't think I have the strength to say much more than, "I don't know what to say…"

"Thank you would be nice," he mutters.

"Thank you," I say sincerely, my own hand inadvertently pressing over my heart. "That means everything to me."

"Whatever," he grumbles. "I'll pay you child support, whatever is standard. And I'll need you to pack up Hope tomorrow. I'd like this done sooner rather than later."

Jesus. Doesn't he care at all about our daughter?

While I don't have a doubt in my mind that this is going to make Hope insanely happy, I know she'll be confused by it, too.

And she'll miss her dad. How could she not?

"Okay. Tomorrow," I murmur into the phone. "Have you told her?"

"You can handle that," he clips out, and then, to my surprise, he hangs up.

I don't care, though. Nothing more to say.

The most important things were said.

I slowly set my phone down, still in a bit of a haze over how drastically and fucking fantastically my life just changed with that phone call.

I rotate on my stool seat to face Asher, who is watching me with what seems to be the keen attention of a hawk. "What did he say?"

My tongue seems thick, and I still don't half believe what I just heard. "Nelson just said he's not fighting me on custody. I can have Hope starting tomorrow. And he'll pay child support."

Asher doesn't say anything, but his eyes sparkle and his lips curl upward.

And then it really hits me, and a jolt of pure joy and awareness of all that is great in my world slams into me.

Grinning hard, I enunciate my words. "He just fucking gave me custody of my daughter."

Asher's smile gets bigger. When I shriek with excitement, he blinks in surprise. Suddenly, I'm throwing myself out of my seat and right at him. I slam into his body, planting my feet on the floor. My arms go around his neck and I start jumping in place as I try to hug him, all the while screaming, "I have custody of Hope. I have custody of Hope."

I feel strong arms come tightly around me, and I'm crushed to his chest as he returns my hug. "That's amazing, Hannah."

God, his voice is so buttery soft and full of happiness on my behalf. It makes me pull away from him so I can check out the expression on his face to see if it matches.

It does, and it makes me feel a little crazy. My hands go to his cheeks, and I plaster my mouth on his.

Asher would never deny my kiss, and he gives it right back to me. Furious and hot and totally taking advantage of my ramped-up excitement right now.

My hand drops to his lap, and I palm his growing erection. Asher growls, lifts me from the stool, and pivots toward the master bedroom. He takes great strides, wanting to minimize the time our mouths are apart.

Wanting to maximize fucking me.

And it's the second-best thing that's happened to me today.

## CHAPTER 21

# *Asher*

I LEAN BACK against my Mercedes, not minding the need to pull it out of the garage and dust it off. While I much prefer the McLaren, it's not practical tonight because it's just a two-seater.

I've been waiting in front of Hannah's house for about fifteen minutes now. She has no clue I'm here because I didn't want to give her a chance to tell me 'no' over the phone.

Just as Hannah is clueless in this moment, so am I. I have no idea why I left work early on a Tuesday night to do something that's so far out of my comfort zone I barely recognize myself these days.

All I do know is I could not let Hannah take her daughter trick or treating in this neighborhood. It's not safe at all.

Why this should bother me is a mystery. My relationship with Hannah took a drastic turn, leaving me with no satisfaction.

Well, that's not quite true. I am beyond satisfied that Nelson did what I told him to do and turned Hope over to Hannah. Fuck, it gave me so much satisfaction after he made that call to Hannah that we had what was the absolute best fucking sex, and it was all because she was riding a wave of pure euphoria. It clearly had a tangential effect on me as well.

Where my dissatisfaction comes into play is that Hannah is no longer mine to do with what I please. I knew this would happen when I went to see Nelson, yet I didn't change course. It's basically my fucking fault I'm in this situation.

Hope moved in with Hannah on Saturday as planned. I know this because Hannah surprised me with a quick text about it. She also told me that her new hours starting Monday would have to be eight-thirty to three since she'd have to take Hope to and from school. Of course, it was implied the evenings were out since she had Hope.

I was aware it would happen, yet it was still a punch to the gut that I'd essentially given up every single night with Hannah. Her priority was now to her daughter.

Sure… I could have had her in the mornings this week. Could have gone to the office late, taking my time with her in my bed. She wouldn't have said no.

But that's not what our arrangement is. I hire her— pay her—to go to a sex club with me. It's gone a little beyond those boundaries for sure, but now everything is changed and I can't expect anything from her.

Which is why it's an absolutely great time to end it with her. Probably tonight after I bring them home.

I'll give her a job in my company, far removed from me so I won't be tempted. She'll still have the same salary, health benefits, and 401K. It's the least I can do for the hours of pleasure—and dare I say happiness— she's brought to me these last several weeks.

Yes, that's what I will do. Hannah and Hope can start a new life together, and I will go back to doing what I do best.

Being alone.

The front door to Hannah's house opens. I lean farther back onto my car, crossing my arms casually as I watch her. She steps out looking fresh, amazing, and happier than I've ever seen her. A little girl comes out next, and she's a fucking "mini-me" of Hannah. Same chestnut hair and smooth complexion. Nose, eyes. There's not a hint of Nelson in her at all.

Hope has her head tipped up to Hannah and is chattering about something. They hold hands as they walk down the porch steps. Hope has on a frothy pink dress with translucent golden wings attached to her back. She's carrying a plastic orange pumpkin bucket to collect candy in.

When they hit the sidewalk, Hannah's head comes up and she sees me. Hope continues to talk to her mother, but Hannah is frozen in place as our eyes lock.

I enjoy her surprise for a moment before she starts moving toward me again. Hope, who has now also seen me standing there, follows along. Pushing off my car, I wait for them to reach me.

My attention goes to Hope, who looks at me with uncertainty. No clue how to fucking talk to kids, but I imagine it can't be that much different than adults.

Right?

Bending slightly, I smile at the little girl. She is totally fucking adorable as she tips her head back to look at me with wide eyes.

"You might be the most beautiful fairy princess I've ever seen."

Hope shyly ducks her head, pressing into Hannah's leg, but she manages to tell me, "Thank you," in a soft voice.

I straighten, bringing my attention to Hannah.

"What are you doing here?" she asks curiously. There's no anger there, which I half expected since I'm here unannounced and uninvited.

"I couldn't in good conscience let you two ladies walk around this neighborhood tonight. It's just too dangerous."

Hannah's tone is amused and skeptical. "So you are what? Going to walk with us to protect us?"

I shake my head and laugh, turning to the rear passenger seat of my car, where I open the door with a flourish. With a charming grin, I announce, "Of course not. I'm going to take you to a super-safe gated neighborhood. Because everyone is rich as sin, they'll have the best candy."

Hope's eyes light up and she peers up at her mom, tugging on the bottom of her thin sweater. "Can we, Mommy?"

Hannah regards me a moment, and I can't believe my fucking heart starts racing in fear that she might decline. But then she glances down at Hope and smiles. "Sure. But let me introduce you first. This is my friend, Mr. Knight."

Hope smiles, still a little shy, but totally charmed by the prospect of premium candy. "Hi."

"Hi," I reply, and then to Hannah. "Let's get in the car and go."

"We need to get her car seat," Hannah says as she points to her car in the small driveway. "Or we could just take mine."

Grimacing, I shake my head. "Not a chance."

It takes us no time at all to get the seat transferred to my car. The hardest part is getting Hope buckled in around the five million layers of fairy princess dress, which is covered in glitter that immediately sheds off onto my seats.

Once we're underway, Hannah asks, "Where are we going?"

"My dad's neighborhood," I say. "He hates any holiday so he'll be hiding inside, but we can park in his driveway and walk from there."

"Cool," Hannah says before twisting in her seat to see Hope. "You okay back there?"

I can see her in my rearview mirror, and Hope gives a toothy smile of adoration to her mom. I knew Hannah was beyond happy to have her daughter back, but it's clear the feeling goes both ways.

Hannah fills me in on her search for a new house in a safer neighborhood. By the time I make it over to my dad's neighborhood, I've resolved myself to pay Hannah more when I move her over to Knight Investment Group so she can afford even better than what she's considering right now.

"Whoa," Hannah gasps as we're given admittance at the guard house. The wrought-iron gates swing slowly inward, and I drive through. "I didn't know houses like this existed."

My guess is this community doesn't have a house that costs less than five million. Most are priced well above it. Every single home has custom landscape lighting, so everything is lit up in a warm, safe glow. The sidewalks are already crawling with other neighborhood rich kids in their costumes.

When I turn onto my dad's street and see his house in the distance, I can't help but hit the brakes to come to a dead stop in the road.

There's my dad's mansion, all white stucco and red-tiled roof—not dark and abandoned looking to ward off trick-or-treaters but blazing with light and decorations.

Orange lights are wrapped around the portico columns and throughout the bushes along the front. The front porch has an impressive display of hay bales, pumpkins, and a full-sized stuffed scarecrow lounging there.

"What the f—?" I catch myself before the F-bomb flies, gaze going quickly to Hannah. "Looks like my dad is home and open for Halloween business."

"Is that a problem?" Hannah asks uneasily.

"Not for our plans tonight," I mutter as I start driving again. "But I might be seriously scarred for life that my dad has started celebrating this holiday."

Hannah snickers, and Hope asks, "What's so funny?"

"Nothing," Hannah reassures her.

We pull into my dad's circular driveway. As we're getting out of the car, a group of trick-or-treaters bound up his porch and ring the doorbell. My jaw drops wide open when I see the door swing open to my dad standing there with a huge sombrero on his head, a Mexican poncho around his shoulders, and a horrendously large black mustache on his face.

"Trick or treat," the kids all yell. My dad laughs, tossing candy in their bags and buckets from a huge bowl. The kids leave, and a woman appears at his side.

His new fiancée, Mandy. She's dressed as a witch. And not a sexy bombshell witch or even Glinda the Good Witch of the North. Nope—she's an old hag-like witch, complete with green skin and a bump on her nose.

Holy shit.

My dad sees me. I can't tell, but I think he smiles underneath that big mustache. I want to jump back in the car and drive away because this is freaking me out so bad. Instead, I walk around the front of the car and offer my hand to Hannah. She's already got Hope out of the car, her other hand touching Hope's back.

As I guide Hannah, she steers Hope forward and up the porch steps to come face to face with a man I no longer recognize.

Metaphorically, of course.

My dad bends over, the little tiny row of colorful pom-poms hanging from his sombrero waving back and forth. "Well, look at you. What's your name?"

"Hope," she says.

Hannah reminds her, "Say trick or treat."

Hope does, and my dad laughs. He immediately proceeds to toss most the bowl of candy in her bucket, filling it almost halfway up.

Straightening, he raises an eyebrow at me expectantly. I jolt into action, remembering my manners. "Dad… this is Hannah Madigan. You've met her daughter, Hope."

I switch my attention to Mandy, who I grudgingly admit I have a small measure of respect for since she managed to get my dad to dress up in that ridiculous costume. "And this is his fiancée, Mandy."

Hannah shakes both their hands graciously, and they exchange pleasantries.

"I thought we'd use your neighborhood to trick or treat in. I'm just going to leave my car in the driveway if that's okay?" I ask my dad.

"Of course, of course," he booms jovially. "And when you're done, come inside and we'll have a drink. Mandy made some Halloween cookies. I bet Hope would love some."

"If it's not too late," I say, vowing silently to make it so. "We better get going."

I usher Hannah and Hope out to the sidewalk and we head down the street to the next property.

"Your dad seems nice," Hannah says, and my head snaps her way.

"That man you just saw... I think he's been overtaken by aliens."

Hannah laughs. "You mean your father isn't normally nice?"

"He's nice enough," I admit. "But dressing up like that? Actually celebrating a holiday? That was just very, very weird."

I get a little smirk from Hannah. "I think it's sweet. I bet his fiancée got him to do it."

That's probably true. There must be some outside force that made such a change in him.

As we traverse the neighborhood, Hope talks excitedly about the other kids and their costumes. I wait at the bottom of each porch as Hannah walks with her to the door, wondering how I ended up in this Twilight Zone.

Taking a woman and her child out trick or treating.

My dad embracing a holiday and dressing up.

My questioning whether I could let Hannah go to Knight Investment Group. It seems a little too magnanimous for such a selfish son of a bitch.

The best thing would be to cut Hannah loose tonight. We'll part as friends, and I can feel proud about my good deeds. I can move on… probably even hit the Wicked Horse tonight and get laid.

For the first time in forever, the thought of going to the club has no appeal to me whatsoever.

I ponder it all as we move from house to house. Hannah eventually lets Hope go up on her own while we wait out on the sidewalk. Her phone stays out, and she has probably taken a million pictures of her daughter already.

She's snapping more as we watch Hope walk up to another door.

"Are you okay?" she unexpectedly asks me, and I jolt.

"Yeah… why?" I ask in surprise.

"You're just really quiet. I don't know… you seem to be struggling with something."

Hannah puts her phone in her pocket before facing me. She moves in closer, her eyebrows pulling in with concern.

Christ, she's beautiful. More so than any other woman I've ever known. It's an inside-and-out sort of beauty, and the thought of not seeing her anymore causes my gut to tighten painfully.

"No," I say after clearing my throat. I give her a reassuring smile. "Nothing's wrong. In fact, I've been wanting to ask you something."

"What's that?" she asks, tilting her head to the side.

*Might as well just fucking go for it.*

"My sister puts on this charity gala, and it's in a few weeks. My mom used to do it and well, Christina has taken up the helm on the project. Would you like to go as my date?"

Hannah just stares at me, obvious confusion written on her face. "Date?"

"You heard me correctly," I say with a smirk, thinking she's so cute right now and it's going to suck not to be able to fuck her tonight.

Hannah worries at her lip with her teeth a moment before she blinds me with a smile. "Okay. But what do I wear? And I need to know when, since I'll need to find a sitter for Hope. Or maybe her dad can take her for the night."

She goes on and on about it, and I assure her that I'll help her with a dress and we'll get everything sorted. We continue to walk from house to house, letting Hope fill her bucket with candy. Out of the blue, Hannah slips her arm through mine as we stroll.

My reflex isn't to push her away. Rather, I instinctually pull her in closer to me.

So this evening isn't ending like I had originally planned, but I think I'm okay with that.

## CHAPTER 22

# *Hannah*

I KNOCK ON Asher's office door, then wait for him to invite me in. Even though he met me at the front door of his apartment this morning when I arrived, and promptly dragged me back to his bedroom for some wild monkey sex, I would never think it's my place to enter one of his rooms with a closed door.

Particularly his office where I know he's doing important things as the CEO of Knight Investment Group.

"You can come in," he calls out genially, and I open the door to stick my head in.

His smile is breathtaking when he sees me. More beautiful now because he smiles at me in a different way.

It's still just as knowing, but there's a softness to it that he's never shown me before.

"I'm done with everything else except your office," I say hesitantly. "I don't want to disturb you, though."

"Your presence in my home disturbs me every minute you're here," he drawls, and my heart plummets over his harsh words. "I can't think straight when I know you're just in the next room over and I could be fucking you."

My eyes go wide, and I swallow hard.

"But," he says with a slow grin curving upward. "That's my problem, not yours. So please… have at it."

He sweeps his arm to show I can come in and attack the interior. I enter the room fully, leaving the door open. I have a carrying bucket with my cleaning supplies, and I pull out my feather duster to start on his custom-built shelves that line the wall behind his desk.

He has a rolling library ladder I use to get to the top shelf. I methodically make my way down the units, getting closer to where he sits. His desk is placed in the middle of the room and his chair is between it and the shelves. I'm going to have to work my way around him, or demand he get out of my way, which is probably the better way.

When I cast a glance at him, I find him lewdly watching me, his eyes pinned on my ass as I bend over to hit a bottom shelf.

"Perv," I mutter, and he laughs.

"I can't help it if your ass is distracting," he murmurs in a husky tone. "So many things I want to do it."

The back of my neck heats, and my nipples tingle. Just this morning, he was riding me from behind and he stuck his index finger in my backside. I'd shrieked from the unexpected burst of pleasure that hit me. I was so embarrassed I tried to get him to stop, but he held me tightly in place. When he started to move that finger in conjunction with his thrusts into me, I went dizzy from the pleasure. It was not like anything I'd ever felt before. Before long, I was throwing myself backward onto him.

Onto his finger.

His cock.

A strong cramp hits me between my legs. I wouldn't fight him at all if he wanted to drag me off to his room again.

I stand, move to the next unit, and start at the top again. When I come down off the ladder, which is now just a foot from Asher's chair, I tell him, "You're going to need to move."

He scoots his chair—which is on rollers—mere inches toward the desk, which is not enough room to get the rolling ladder by him.

I glare at him, and he smirks.

"Fine," I say under my breath as I turn to face his desk. He keeps it pristine with documents neatly stacked in wooden trays and barely any knickknacks taking up the surface. I hit it with my feather duster, feeling Asher's stare on me the entire time. I choose to go around the front of the desk rather than maneuvering behind him. When I get to the other side, he says, "Any chance I could get you to sit on my lap while you dust my desk?"

Biting back a smile, I try to look professionally stern as I swish my duster over the dark cherry surface. "Mr.

Knight… that's sexual harassment."

"So sue me," he taunts before suggesting, "Or… we could get naked."

"Not interested," I tell him—untruthfully—and pivot for the bookshelves again.

Asher's hand shoots out, latching around my stomach, and he pulls me right onto his lap as he suggested. Screaming with laughter, I try to wiggle away. I can feel the thick ridge of him under my thighs, and he snatches the duster out of my hand while tightening his hold on me.

"You know," he says in a playful voice. "I bet I could make you come with this thing."

*Oh, man. Really?*

But I'm not ready to roll over and expose my belly so to speak. I try to snatch the duster back from him. He's too quick and moves it out of the way. I lunge, faster than he gives me credit for, and my hand latches onto a fistful of feathers. I jerk hard. To my surprise, my hand sails back clutching a massive amount of brownish-gray feathers.

The force causes my arm to fly all the way across his desk, and it hits against something.

I hear a crash. As I turn to see what I just knocked to the floor, my stomach knots in horror as I see it was the picture of his dead wife and him. It lays face down on the hardwood floor, but I know it's the one with Michelle. It's the only picture he has in this office.

"Oh, Jesus," I moan as I scramble off Asher's lap. He makes this easy by releasing his hold on me. I kneel and gingerly pick up the frame. Glass falls loose onto the floor. I turn it over to see Michelle smiling back at me with some larger pieces of cracked glass still hanging onto the inside.

I turn to look at Asher, feeling like I'm going to throw up. "I am so sorry, Asher."

He just sits in his chair, staring a little blankly at the picture frame in my hand. My stomach knots even more.

"The picture is okay," I rush to assure him, glancing back down at it one more time to reassure myself that it is. And it is. The picture inside looks unscathed. My gaze goes back to Asher. "I can run out right now and buy another frame. I'm sure I can find one just like it. Christ... first the Chihuly and now this. I'm such a klutz."

I'm startled when Asher reaches out. He doesn't take the picture from my hand, but rather grabs my free hand. He squeezes it, giving me a soft, forgiving smile. "It's okay, Hannah."

"I feel terrible," I say weakly.

Asher stands from the chair and takes the frame. I release it gladly. Without even looking at it, he sets it on the desk and then pulls me into him.

His arms come around my waist, his head dipping so he can brush his lips across mine. My entire body wants to melt in relief. I feel like I could use a good wailing cry.

"I swear it's fine," he says after pulling back to look at me.

We stare at each other a moment, and I desperately search for some sign within his expression that he's truly okay with this. His gaze doesn't waver, and I'm slightly mollified.

Stepping out of his arms, I say, "Let me go get a broom and dust pan to clean up this glass."

Asher smiles and nods. "Sure."

I scurry to the door. Just as I'm about to walk through, I look over my shoulder at him. He's turned to the desk and is picking up the frame. My heart seems to stall in my chest as he rubs a thumb over the edge while he stares at his dead wife.

Then, he pulls open a side drawer of the desk and puts it in there. I get the hell out of there before he finds me spying on him.

It should take me less than thirty seconds to get the broom and dust pan, but I'm still a little shaken by the whole incident. I grab a bottle of water from the fridge and drink half of it before I have myself calmed down enough to go back into his office.

With my implements in hand, I make my way back there. The door is still open. Asher sits behind his desk again, packing up papers into a briefcase.

Without looking at me, he says, "I'm going to go into the office for the rest of the afternoon."

"Okay," I murmur in response.

Is he mad? Morose? Indifferent? I can't tell.

I make quick work of sweeping up the glass from the floor, then dump it into the garbage can by his desk.

"I'm really sorry," I feel the need to apologize again, wondering if the status of this budding relationship just took a major hit.

Asher stands from his chair. Again, I get another smile—genuine and understanding. "Hannah… don't apologize again. You hurt nothing. Do you understand me?"

I nod although it's not clear if he's talking about the frame, himself, or both.

He holds my gaze with his for what seems like a pointedly long moment, and then he bowls me over with his next words. "It was time I put that picture away."

"Oh, no," I rush to assure him, stepping in close and putting the hand still clutching the dust pan to his chest. "I would never want you to feel like you had to put away a picture of the woman you love just to make me feel better about the whole thing."

A twinkle of amusement lights up his eyes, and he bends down to put his face on level with mine. So now, he's not looking down at me, but rather right at me. It's a move that says, *I'm being serious so listen well.*

His hand comes to my face. He uses it to take hold of my jaw, the implication being that I can't look away from him.

"I did love Michelle," he says in the softest of tones,

yet its shot through with an iron strength of determination. "But that's not why I've kept her picture out five years after her death. I had it out as a reminder that you never truly know someone."

"I don't understand," I whisper as I lower my hand and the dust pan away from his chest.

For a moment, his expression turns pained, causing me to want to throw my arms around him. He grimaces and sighs. Setting his briefcase down, he leans back against his desk and crosses his arms.

"Michelle had some bouts of depression," he explains. I feel ridiculous standing there with a broom in one hand and the dust pan in the other, but I'm rooted to the spot. "She took medication for it. I assumed it was working because not in a million years would I have ever thought she was in such a dark place that she'd kill herself. I've tortured myself since then, Hannah, wondering what I missed. How I missed it. Was I stupid or just naïve? Or was she just so fucking great at hiding it? What if I should have seen it, though? What if it was right there in front of me and I just missed it because I was so wrapped up in work or myself or what the fuck ever?"

"I can't imagine the guilt you've felt," I murmur sorrowfully. "I wish I could say or do something to alleviate that for you, but I don't know what to do."

He shakes his head. "You can't do anything. It's on me to deal with it. I've kept that picture as a reminder of the pain I felt when I found her. Of the anger I felt because I was pissed at her. As a reminder that I won't ever get in that position again."

I don't know what to say to this. I mean, these are the sorts of things I knew about Asher. He's withdrawn from life to some extent, and he's closed himself off to so many things that could put his emotions at risk of hurt.

I lay it out there, so he knows I understand. "You've cut yourself off from relationships, so you won't get hurt again. It's why you go to a sex club. Why you wanted to keep distance from me. I understand it. I really do."

We stare at each other a moment while the words hang in the air.

Then, Asher steps into me, sliding one hand to the back of my neck. Peering down at me, he asks, "Do you think you could free up a night sometime in the next week to have a night out with me? And I'm not talking about to the club. I was thinking dinner. Maybe a movie."

An amazing feeling of hope and light fills me that this man is really putting his past in a drawer and is taking that first tentative step outside of the fortress he's built up around himself.

"Yes," I tell him with a firm nod of my head. "Nelson is going to take Hope from Saturday morning until Sunday afternoon, so if that works for you?"

"It works great," he says, and then his mouth is on mine. It's so atypical of the type of hot kissing we normally engage in. It's thoughtful, somewhat hesitant, and yet there's no mistaking the yearning within it.

My chest constricts, and I am fully aware I've fallen for this man. I have to admit it now—at least to myself—since he's taken the huge step of opening up to me.

And despite the hell I went through getting out of my marriage with Nelson, and with being bullied and intimidated by him, I don't find myself hesitant at all in giving myself to Asher. I trust that he will not hurt me the way Nelson did.

I just don't think he has it in him, to be honest.

My arms go around his neck. While I make the kiss no sexier than what it is, I want him to feel from it that I'm ready for him to take that risk with me.

# CHAPTER 23

## *Asher*

HANNAH'S PUSSY SQUEEZES my dick so hard I believe she might be coming again. That knowledge sends me over the edge, and I plant deep inside of her before I explode.

My forehead drops to hers and I groan out the release, relishing the ripples of pleasure that roll up my spine.

"Goddamn," I huff out as I let some of my body weight down onto her.

Those beautiful eyes of hers flutter open, locking right onto me. One corner of her mouth pulls up into a smirk. "You outdid yourself that time."

I can feel my ego swelling. "Did you come a third time?"

She nods with a dopey grin on her face. It makes me laugh as I gather her in my arms and roll us to the side.

We're practically nose to nose as we settle in, still trembling and huffing from that marathon of a fuck-fest.

Christ, I think Hannah has completely ensnared me into her web of sexuality laced sweetness. I'm pretty confident sex with anyone else would be so lackluster I'd want to become a monk.

"Stay the night?" I ask.

"Okay," she replies with a tiny smile. My arms squeeze her to me a little tighter.

Tonight was perfect. Despite the fact we've been having sex for weeks, I was still anxious over what would be our first true date. It had all felt a bit new to me.

Nelson had picked up Hope this morning, and Hannah spent most of the day looking at new housing for them. I spent the day watching the clock tick by while working at the office because I have no life and nothing better to do.

And then it was time for our date, and the evening was a revelation.

Hannah dressed up—classy, not sexy—and looked magical. We had an amazing dinner that lasted almost three hours, not because the food was slow but because the conversation was never ending. While I've been able to put together bits and pieces of Hannah over the last several weeks, I finally got the complete picture tonight.

Let me tell you… she's a force to be reckoned with.

She grew up dirt poor in rural South Carolina with an absentee father and a mother who worked her hands to the bone to put food on the table. Hannah had to work at an early age while helping to raise her siblings.

She told me she felt incredible guilt when she met Nelson, had a whirlwind romance, and then realized that meant she'd have to move back to Vegas where he was from. She felt terrible leaving her family behind.

Throughout it all, the one thing they were never lacking was love. It's an interesting juxtaposition to my family. We had all the money in the world and lived a lavish lifestyle, yet we weren't overly close as a unit. Sure, our mother was loving, and Christina and I were close because we're twins, but that was it. I can tell, though... Hannah, her mom, and her brothers were a team.

She misses them terribly. Had it not been for Nelson insisting Hope stay here, she would have gone back with her daughter.

To my surprise, Hannah declined my suggestion we see a movie after dinner. I was trying to do a classic first date, but Hannah was done with it.

"Let's go to your place and get naked," she murmured in my ear as we were standing outside the valet stand at the restaurant waiting for my car. She was tucked into my side, both of her arms wrapped around my one. "We've not had a lot of time together, and I miss you."

A bolt of lust hit me, and something inside my chest seemed to stretch and awaken. Hannah missed sex with me, but I believe she also just missed *me*. Our time together this week on her new schedule was sparse for sure.

She was able to put into a few simple, honest words how I had been feeling. I had missed her, too.

So here we are, having just achieved maximum orgasms, and I'm not sure why I deserve this goodness in my life right now. I fucked up my first real relationship and never asked for a second chance. Yet, here it is, and I've tentatively reached for it.

"Asher," Hannah murmurs, pulling me out of my reminiscence. I focus in on her beautiful face. "How upset would you be if I looked for another job?"

"You mean a second job?" I ask curiously. "Do you need more money?"

"No," she says as her eyes cut sideways a second before coming back to me. "A whole new job. Not working for you."

This is shocking, and it causes me to rise to an elbow so I can look down at her with better clarity. "Don't you like what you do?"

"That's a loaded question," she replies as she props herself up, putting her on equal footing with me as we stare at each other. "This basically started as sex for money, plain and simple. We've couched it in terms of a job, and sure, I clean your place because I can't fuck you forty hours a week."

"That would be great if you could," I point out.

She grins and brings a hand to my chest, where she presses her palm to my skin. "You're not paying me for sex anymore, though. We've moved past that, but I can't in good conscience take that type of money from you for twenty hours a week cleaning your place. It feels... wrong."

I blink, hating what she says but also understanding it. Hannah has pride. She's got an incredible work ethic. She's not the type who wants a white knight swooping in and pulling her up from despair. She'd rather just have him reach a hand out and give her a little boost, which I've already done.

To continue would be degrading to her self-esteem.

I get it.

"Hannah," I say gently. "You can't make that type of money somewhere else with just one job. You'd have to go back to three. That's impossible as you have Hope."

"Well, I can't let you be my sugar daddy," she snaps with a fierce glare.

"God, you're fucking adorable when you're mad," I say before I plant a swift, hard kiss to her mouth.

She glares harder, and I laugh. "What if I were to offer you a job at Knight Investment Group that would be comparable with the salary you're making? I'd also offer you and Hope health and dental as well as a 401K."

I get more blinking, but it doesn't stop and goes beyond just surprise. Before I know it, she's blinking back tears.

"Oh no," I say in a panic, placing a hand on her shoulder and patting her awkwardly. "Oh no you don't. Don't start crying on me."

"I'm sorry," she sniffs as she wipes at her cheeks. "It's just... I could never thank you enough for the opportunities you've given me. It's because of you I have my daughter back."

Hannah really doesn't know just how true that is because I've never told her about my deal with Nelson, and he's clearly not said anything to her.

I can't stand to see the pure, raw emotion on her face. It's too much to handle, so I pull her back into my arms and tuck her face into my chest where I let her cry for a bit.

"Will you accept my offer?" I ask.

Hannah pulls back, her eyes still a little shiny but I can tell she's back in control. "I'm not qualified for much, Asher. I've got some basic secretarial skills, which is what I did until we had Hope. Then I was a stay-at-home mom."

"Then I'll find you a basic secretarial job within the company," I assure her.

"Not at what you're paying me, though," she says with a shake of her head. "I'm actually getting good child support from Nelson, so I don't have to make that type of salary."

"Not budging on that, Hannah," I tell her firmly. "It's what you're paid now, and what you've given me has been worth ten times as much."

"Orgasms aren't worth that much," she says dryly.

"You know fucking good and well I'm not talking

about orgasms," I say quietly. "Just accept the offer as is and let's move on, okay?"

She nibbles at her lip. Of course, that makes me want to fuck her again. But I wait patiently for her answer. An idea seems to strike her. "Maybe I could still clean your place on the weekends or something?"

One of my eyebrows arches, and I just stare at her.

"Okay, maybe not," she amends.

"Just say yes," I order.

"And if I don't?" she challenges, a spark of defiance in her eyes that turns me on.

"You get the palm of my hand," I tell her ominously.

"Then I most definitely will not say yes," she says with a smile, and that's all I need to hear. I crush my mouth to hers, pulling back to bite at her lip.

"Going to redden your ass good," I promise.

"God, I hope so," she purrs in return.

# CHAPTER 24

# *Hannah*

I PULL A hanger holding a lavender-colored shift dress that I've had since before Hope was born out of my closet. I think I bought it to attend a spring picnic at Nelson's company.

I'm fairly sure the style is still relevant, and it's in decent shape since I've only worn it a handful of times over the years. Incredibly lucky to have lost all the weight I'd gained with my pregnancy, I don't bother to try it on. Instead, I move to the bed and lay it across the top of the pile of clothes I'll keep.

I'm moving this weekend to a new apartment. After which, I'll start my new job at Knight Investment Group on Monday. I'm terrified and thrilled at the same time. And it's sad to say, but at the age of twenty-seven, I'm finally feeling like a full-fledged adult. I'm single momming it with Hope and I'll be working in a professional job, which gives me a nice boost to my self-esteem. Another thing I'm grateful to Asher for.

"Mommy," Hope says as she comes into my bedroom, holding up one of her dolls. "I can't find her pink dress with the sparkly stuff on it."

"Hope," I say in a stern voice as I turn back to my closet. "You're supposed to be putting your toys into the boxes."

My daughter walks to my bed, finds a space without clothing, and flops down dramatically. "It's so hard to pack. Can you help me?"

Since my back is to Hope, I can let loose the amused smile that comes to my face. I really didn't expect her to do much, but I thought it was good to give her some responsibility in helping with the move.

But bottom line... she's five and would rather play than pack, and that's something I'm cool with. I don't want her growing up too fast on me.

"I'll help you finish tomorrow as it's getting close to your bedtime," I say as I pull out a floral-print skirt in pastel colors. How did I end up with such light colors in my closet? Was I a sweet and timid woman, which is how this clothing is making me feel?

I personally feel like I'm more edgy.

Definitely sexy after some of the clothing that Asher has had me wear to The Wicked Horse.

Still, I put it in the "keep" pile. I need to have as many "work" clothes as I can because I can't afford a new wardrobe.

Turning to Hope, I say, "Go brush your teeth and

get your jammies on."

"Okay," she chirps and hops off the bed. She clutches her doll under one arm, the pink sparkle dress completely forgotten.

"Thanks, honey," I murmur as she runs out of my room. I'm not sure if all kids are like this but Hope always seems to run to wherever she's going, especially if she's on a mission. Perhaps that's a sign of motivation.

I pull out a few more outfits, deem one to be worthy of keeping and put two into the donation pile. It's a pain in the ass to have to pack up this house, but I'm using the opportunity to purge a lot of stuff. I'm lightening up because I've got a fresh start.

The apartment I found is incredible. It's about ten minutes from my new job and fifteen minutes closer to Asher. It's in a great school district and by all reviews, it's quiet and safe.

Leaving my packing, I head down to Hope's room. I like to get her to sleep by eight, but it takes a bit of unwinding so I have her jammied up and teeth brushed by seven thirty. Our bedtime ritual is always the same.

My daughter scrambles under the covers and I pull them up to her chest, tucking them in tight around her.

"Mommy," Hope says in a tone that says something's on her mind.

"What's up, buttercup?" I reply playfully.

She doesn't smile. Instead, she asks in a hesitant voice, "Will I have to go back and live with Daddy?"

"You mean like full time?"

She nods, her face a mix of hope and fear.

"I don't think so, honey," I tell her carefully. "You're with me now, but you'll visit Daddy on some nights."

"I don't want to go back there to live," she says fiercely. "He never pays attention to me. Always just has me watch TV while he works or talks to his girlfriends."

I internally wince at the plural of "girlfriend" as I know Nelson has had a revolving door and it was confusing to Hope.

"And if he's not working or with a girlfriend, he's always looking at his phone," she continues.

What in the hell is wrong with my ex? How could he think anything in the world was more important or interesting than his own daughter? I could just stare at her for hours while she slept, because that's better than anything else I could ever be doing.

"I won't let it happen," I vow to her. "You're with me forever. You'll still spend time with Daddy each week, but your home is with me, okay?"

"Okay," she says with a relieved smile, and I hope I can keep that promise. I have no clue if Nelson would ever go back on his deal with me, but I would bleed for my daughter not to go back to him. I think he loves her, but not the way I do.

"Make your picks," I tell her, and she names the three books she wants me to read tonight.

After I massage her imagination with tales of princesses, Pooh, and wild things, I turn out her bedside lamp. Her room still glows as we have two night lights plugged in and she wants her bedroom door open and the hall light left on.

Ever since Hope was a baby, I've sang her to sleep. I don't have the best voice in the world, but it's apparently soothing as she usually barely makes it three songs before she's out.

Settling onto the side of her bed, I place my hand on her chest as I start to sing. She always watches me carefully with big solemn eyes. Her lips curve into a sleepy smile, and I'm no more than a few lines into the third song before her eyes grow heavy and close. I continue singing until I hear that deep steady breathing that shows she's out, and then I lean over and brush my lips against her forehead.

I will never, ever take this time with her for granted. It's the most special part of my day.

Quietly standing from Hope's bed, I ease out into the hallway. Just as I'm back in my closet, looking at the next outfit, I hear a knock on the door. It's sharp and demanding.

I go cold for a moment because in the year I've been living here, no one has ever come to my door after dark apart from that one night Asher came by when I was sick. The wise people in this neighborhood go indoors at night, and the only ones out usually are the troublemakers.

Without hesitation, I retrieve my shotgun out of the locked cabinet in my closet and quickly check to ensure it's loaded. I know it is, but still… always check.

Padding softly to the door, I quietly lean in and put my eye up to the peep hole. My entire body relaxes all at once to see it's not a gang member—not that they'd ever knock on my door if they wanted something—but rather my ex-husband.

I unlock the door and open it. "What are you doing here?" I ask curiously, then move to the side as a silent invitation to enter.

"I came by to see Hope." Nelson rolls his eyes when he sees the gun. I ignore his dismissal of my need for security and say, "I'll be right back."

It takes me just a few moments to put the gun back in the cabinet and return to the living room. This is the first time Nelson has ever been to my home.

I find him surveying the boxes I'd already packed up.

"Hope's sleeping, and I don't want to wake her," I tell him. He pivots towards me, and I add, "And it would be nice if you called ahead of time. It's disconcerting to have someone knocking on my door at night when I'm not expecting anyone."

He doesn't acknowledge my request, just says, "Looks like you're moving."

"Yeah," I reply with a sigh. Same old Nelson, not even listening to me. "An apartment in a better neighborhood now that I can afford to."

"Because of my hefty child support," he grouses.

I let it go, choosing not to fight with him. It's just not worth it, and I don't want to ever rock the boat.

Nelson's gaze moves past me into the kitchen, which is also covered in boxes—some packed, some empty. The counters are covered with all the pots, pans, and dishes I'd pulled out to pack.

His face hardens, and I know what he's locked eyes on.

The flowers I received today from Asher. And not just any flowers, but a massive bouquet of stargazer lilies and freesia that smells divine.

"Now who could be sending you flowers?" he muses out loud in an almost suspicious tone as he brushes past me. I sigh with impatience as I watch him stalk into the kitchen. What the hell does Nelson have to be suspicious of? We've been divorced for over a year, and I'm well within my right to date. Moreover, I can't figure out why he would care. He's moved on to other women.

I hold my tongue because with Hope sleeping just down the hall, I don't want wake her. She's seen enough of her parents fighting to last a lifetime, and I don't want to subject her to it anymore if I can help it.

Nelson snatches the card off to read, and my skin flushes.

Not with embarrassment that he's reading it, but because of the actual words that were written. It's the same flush I felt when I read it this afternoon when they were delivered. The warmth it produced was unlike any I'd felt before.

Ever.

And I felt cherished beyond measure. I also realized Asher was making a very concerted effort to "date" me, even though it wasn't something he'd aspired to do. Hell, he's even going to help Hope and me move on Saturday, which I never asked him to do. In his bossy way, he merely told me he was going to come help.

Nelson's eyes roam the words on the card, and I can see them in my memory since I'd read it probably a dozen times.

*I'm missing you. Thought you should know. Asher.*

"I knew it," he says in triumph as he tosses the card on the table.

"Knew what?" I ask, completely confused.

"That you were fucking Asher Knight," he says, and it is in a totally gloating way. He's clearly not jealous or offended. He almost sounds like a guy who has bet money on something.

"I'm sorry… what?" I manage to say, just not understanding what's going on.

Nelson swaggers toward me, his face a mask of superiority. "Your boyfriend came to one of my jobsites the week before last and offered me a guaranteed project on one of his properties if I agreed not to fight you on custody."

There's no stopping the way gravity pulls my jaw

downward.

Nelson seems to think it's awesome that he gets to inform me of some perfidy Asher has committed. "He told me you were a 'valued' employee, but I knew that smelled like bullshit. No one leverages millions of dollars for a goddamn secretary or whatever the hell you do for him."

*Oh, Nelson... if only you knew what my job actually entails.*

He smugly stares down at me. "What do you think about that?"

I tap my finger to my chin and gaze up to the ceiling thoughtfully, as if I'm putting effort into pondering how egregious this might be.

When I bring my eyes back to Nelson, I say, "To be honest, I find it incredibly sexy he'd do that for me. I'm going to have to give him a very big thank you when I see him."

Nelson's complexion goes from white to purple, totally bypassing red. He opens his mouth to say something, then closes it because nothing comes to mind. I can see it in his eyes... he's offended I'm not offended.

But why would I be? Asher did something so incredibly thoughtful to save me a world of misery. I could never be mad. I might be a little worried since he now has to do business with Nelson, but I figure Asher is a big boy. Besides, if there was a battle between these two men, I'd wager everything on Asher.

"So typical of you, Hannah," Nelson spits out before pivoting on his foot to leave. He stomps through the house, then pulls the door open.

"Call next time before you come over," I call out after him.

He flips me the bird over his shoulder before walking out and slamming the door behind him. I wince and hold still to see if it woke Hope. I don't hear anything, so I mosey to the door and lock it.

My phone is in the kitchen, so I go grab it. I sit down at the table where I can smell the fragrance of the gorgeous flowers Asher thought to send me.

I dial him and settle in, waiting for him to answer. It only takes two rings before his rich, sexy, and confident voice says, "This is a surprise."

What's even better, it sounds like he's happy about it.

"Nelson came over," I say. "He felt the need to tell me how you offered him a project if he wouldn't fight the custody."

"Asshole," Asher mutters.

"You didn't have to do that." My words are soft but filled with emotion.

"It was nothing," he asserts. "I just figured to speed up the process of what I'm sure was going to be the same outcome."

"But you gave him a huge project," I say, the worry

in my voice clear.

"Your husband may be a douche, but his work is good. My company has contracted with him before, so I wasn't risking much."

"It's a bit of a risk," I point out, looking at my flowers. "I'm afraid he might do something shitty because you're involved with me. He saw the flowers. Read the card. He wasn't happy."

"I don't give a fuck if it has his panties in a twist," Asher growls. "And if he's got a problem with it, he needs to man up and come see me. But otherwise, I only care what you think."

"Well," I drawl in a sexy voice. "If you must know, receiving them was the highlight of my day. So thank you again."

I'd already called him earlier when they were delivered. He didn't pick up—probably in a meeting—so I hung up and sent a text thanking him instead. He texted me back, *In a meeting, glad you liked.*

I'd smiled, holding the phone and his words to my chest a moment. The ding of another text had me pulling it back.

*More to come*, he wrote.

I sighed like a swoony princess falling hard over her prince.

Or knight as the case may be.

"Are you going to be at the apartment in the morning when I get there?" I ask.

"Yeah, why?" he replies, no hiding the interest in his voice.

Lowering my voice, I purr into the phone. "Stay in bed and be naked, okay?"

His voice is gruff. "I can do that."

"Good," I say softly. "Because I intend to give you a really big thank you for what you did with Nelson and getting Hope back for me so quickly. I hope you can handle it."

His husky laugh of appreciation tells me that oh yeah… he's going to like it a lot.

# CHAPTER 25

## *Asher*

"M-O-M-M-M-M-Y," Hope yells from her new bedroom. "I need help."

Hannah and I are standing side by side at the L-shaped kitchen counter, each with our own box of stuff to unpack.

I'm more than pleased with Hannah's choice of place to live. It's in a much safer area, and she'll be a little closer to me.

"What do you need?" Hannah calls as she shoots me a side grin.

I reach into my box and pull out a stack of plates that are individually wrapped in newspaper. Sitting them on the counter, I start to unwrap each one, dropping the paper to the floor. I listen to Mom and daughter converse back and forth.

"My iPad," Hope yells. "It's stuck."

"Are you trying to buy something in the App store?"

There's a long pause. "Um… never mind. I figured it

out."

Hannah laughs. "I thought Nelson was crazy for buying a five-year-old an iPad, but admittedly there's a lot of neat learning games on there."

"What's she trying to buy? Porn?" I ask.

When Hannah shakes her head, her ponytail swings back and forth, making her look like a teenager. All makeup scrubbed from her face and wearing a ratty t-shirt with shorts cut from sweatpants and feet bare. Sexy as fuck. "The games have levels. To advance, you have to buy it."

Makes sense. It's all about monetizing.

As for Hope and the iPad, I have no clue whether it's appropriate or not. I don't know much when it comes to kids.

"So," I drawl a bit hesitantly, which gets Hannah's attention. She shifts to look at me. "What does Hope think about this thing between us?"

"This thing between us?" she teases with a grin.

She gets a censuring smirk back from me. I return to unwrapping the plates. "Yeah... I mean... what does she know about me? And you? As in together? Like, should I refrain from giving you affection in front of her? I don't want her to feel threatened by me, especially since you living full time together is kind of new again."

Hannah doesn't answer so I give her my attention. She's staring at me with a dopey smile on her face.

"What?" I ask.

She shakes her head, putting a hand on my forearm. "It's just... that you would even care to ask... Or that you just inherently know that could be an issue with a kid. Her own dad never got that."

"So we play it very cool for a while," I suggest.

She doesn't respond directly. "When I got the flowers from you, she asked who they were from. I told her they were from you, and she wanted to know right away if we were getting married."

My eyebrows shoot up so high and fast that Hannah laughs.

"Relax," she croons with a jab to my ribs. "At her age, all women are princesses and they get swept up by their true love and get married. She doesn't understand what dating is, but she's a smart girl. She'll figure it out."

I lean over and give her a kiss on her neck. "So we'll definitely play it cool."

"No hot kissing or heavy petting in her presence," she says with a glitter in her eyes.

"I'll follow your lead," I mutter dryly.

"Welcome to 'dating a single mom'."

"I'm up for the challenge," I warn.

She gives me a warm smile. "I'm glad."

Grabbing her empty box, Hannah carries it into the living room where she breaks it down and lays it on a pile of flattened cardboard we'd started.

"I'm going to go look for the box that has all the sheets so I can make the beds," she informs me. "It's going to be time for Hope's bedtime soon."

I nod. "Go. I can finish the kitchen. And maybe after Hope falls asleep, we can fool around?"

"Damn right we will," she replies tartly, then blows me a kiss before disappearing down the hall.

I finish the box of dishes and move on to one containing glassware. I'm halfway through when Hope comes in, glancing at me shyly. The night I took her and her mom trick or treating, she'd warmed up to me significantly, fueled by the magical excitement of the evening and tons of candy.

But today, it's kind of starting over again, and we've never talked by ourselves. Frankly, I'm a bit terrified because if the kid hates me, Hannah and I are done. I know enough about her as a mother that it must work out between me and Hope if it's going to work out between me and Hannah.

I've figured it out these last few weeks, and I absolutely want to see where this goes with her.

I decide to face the situation. Try to develop a rapport with her child. "Need any help with the iPad?" I ask Hope as she walks to the fridge and opens it.

"No," she says in a lilting voice. "Mom won't let me buy stuff on there."

That conversation falls flat. But because I'm an entrepreneur and I got my successes from diving right into the deep end, plus flexing the power of money, I decide to take the same tact with Hope.

"What are some of the fun things around here that you might like to do?" I ask. "Maybe I can take you and your mom somewhere next weekend."

She shrugs and pulls a bottle of water out of the fridge, which is all that's in there except for a pizza box with the two slices that were left from our dinner.

"How about the Hoover Dam?" I suggest.

Another shrug, but definitely a slight wrinkle to her nose at the suggestion.

"Hiking?"

She shakes her head.

"A hockey game?" I suggest.

Another shrug with enough disinterest in her expression to tell me I'm completely on the wrong path.

I have a slight moment of panic that maybe I can't do this, but then it strikes me. "How about Disneyland? Ever been there?"

This time, Hope's eyes widen and sparkle with excitement. "Really?"

"Sure," I say with a casual smile. It would be an easy weekend trip to Anaheim.

But just as quickly, Hope's face clouds over. "My dad always had a girlfriend around, and he never paid attention to me."

Something about that strikes deep because I can relate in a way. My dad was wrapped up in business and pretty much ignored me and Christina for much of our formative years. Luckily, I had a wonderful mother who more than made up for it, so I know in that way Hope can relate.

I kneel in front of her, get eye to eye. "Your mother loves you more than anything on this earth, and that will never happen. You will always be first with her. I'm okay with that, just so you know. Okay?"

She nods, looking a bit flustered.

"I'll never take her away from you. I respect you and your mom too much to do that. And if you don't want me along, you tell your mom and she'll respect that, too."

Hope considers what I said, and then dips her head to look at me shyly. "I think you should come to Disneyland with us, though."

I laugh, because she doesn't understand she's not going to be able to go without me since I'd be paying for it. But I keep that to myself because she never needs to know that. Instead, I extend my fist out for her to bump. She curls her tiny hand and taps it against mine.

Hannah bustles into the living room, looks at us over the island that separates it from the kitchen, and dumps more cardboard. I stand up, and she arches an eyebrow.

"What are you two talking about?" she asks while narrowing a fake suspicious look at us.

I shrug, but Hope gives us up. "Asher is going to take us to Disneyland next weekend."

"What?" Hannah gasps, shooting me a look of disbelief laced with censure.

I decide to own it. It will get me in faster with Hope anyway. "Quick weekend trip. On me. It will be fun."

Hannah purses her lips, shaking her head at me in mock disapproval for not discussing it with her first. Then she turns to her daughter. "I suppose we could go if your dad will agree to it."

"Yay," Hope screeches. To my surprise, she throws her arms around my waist and gives me a quick hug. My hand drops and awkwardly pats her on the head.

"Okay, come on, bug," Hannah says to her daughter, holding her hand out. "Let's get you into your jammies. I have your bed made, and it's time to get to sleep. Say goodnight to Asher."

Hope tips her head back and grins at me. "Goodnight, Asher."

"Goodnight, Hope," I murmur back as she runs to join her mom, feeling like I'm on a good path right now with her. So what if I bought my way there.

"Be back in a little bit," Hannah says as she starts leading Hope away. Then she looks over her shoulder and gives a pointed nod to the couch. "Meet you there."

My mouth curves into an evil smile, and I wonder what things I can do to her that would not be a danger to waking Hope up.

I'm determined to finish the kitchen before Hannah returns, and there's only four boxes left. I dig in, removing tape and paper around breakable objects. I make decisions on where her cutlery should be stored and which cabinets to place all the plates and bowls. If she doesn't like it, I'll move it later.

I make it to the last box, which is smaller than the other ones and a lot lighter. It says in black sharpie on the front, "Odds and Ends – Kitchen".

Peeling the packing tape off, I open the flaps. It's a hodgepodge of stuff that Hannah apparently threw in there that belonged in the kitchen but weren't big enough or breakable enough to be wrapped.

I start pulling stuff out, putting everything where I think appropriate. A set of screwdrivers, a measuring tape, a small plastic spoon holder, a set of dish towels, a cork screw, birthday candles, matches, toothpicks, and tons of magnets that go on the fridge. At the bottom of the box, there's a piece of paper folded in half that I imagine she'd had stuck to her fridge with a magnet.

Without thought, I flip it over and read it.

It's an appointment reminder for Hannah from Las Vegas Hematology and Oncology set for week after next. I stare at it a moment before I grab a magnet and stick it to the fridge. I continue to stare at it with an almost dispassionate eye, refusing to believe Hannah could be sick in any way.

"Okay... she's asleep. Went right down, tired little monkey."

I glance over my shoulder at Hannah as she comes into the kitchen. She grins and slides up to me, putting her arms around my waist from behind. Resting her chin on my shoulder, she teases, "Want to make out?"

It's the furthest thing from my mind right now. I point at the appointment reminder I just put on the fridge. "Why do you have that appointment?"

Hannah steps around me with a frown to see the paper. She smiles, as if there's not a care in the world. "It's just a routine follow-up. Nothing big."

"Follow-up for what?" I ask, my voice clipped and filled with tension. I can't quite explain the feeling of dread inside of me, but it's starting to overwhelm me.

The smile drops off Hannah's face when she realizes I'm upset. She softens her tone, as if it will ease the weight of her news. "I was diagnosed with Hodgkin's Lymphoma three years ago. It was the earliest stage and very treatable."

My teeth involuntarily grind together. It's a visible sign of upset to Hannah so she tries to soothe me. "I'm completely fine now. My prognosis is excellent. I feel the best I've ever felt."

"Except your immune system is a little shot," I accuse.

Brow furrowing, she's hesitant in her response. "Yes. I told you that."

"But you didn't tell me why, did you Hannah?" I clip out. "How come you never told me this?"

"It didn't come up," she says defensively.

"It's cancer for God's sake," I snap. "It should have been brought up. By you."

Hannah flushes red. Narrowing her eyes, she steps into me, speaking in a low, cold tone. "Listen, Asher. For four weeks, all we did was fuck and I cleaned your house. I was your paid whore. You took me on our first date last week, and we talked for three hours. I'm sorry, but that's just not enough time to cover my entire life. It never came up. I didn't think it was important enough to bring up as I'm in remission and I'm doing fine. I don't get why this is such a big problem."

"How can you minimize this?" I ask, astounded.

"Maybe because it was never a big deal," she snarls, keeping her voice low. "I had a small child and a husband who didn't seem to care I had a disease. I drove myself, with Hope in tow no less, for chemo for four months. I had a family back home I didn't want to worry, so I didn't let them know I was doing it all on my own. I went through it with only Hope for comfort, so maybe you might understand a little why I don't share. It's something I've had to minimize in my mind so I could get through it."

She's breathing hard, her eyes flaming with anger and righteous indignation.

"Christ, you married a douche," is all I can think to say as I step back from her and scrub my fingers through my hair in agitation.

"Agreed," she clips out. "But I can't seem to figure out why you're mad at me about this?"

I shake my head, disgruntled and off kilter. "I'm

not."

"You clearly are," she retorts.

"You should have told me." It's the only thing I can seem to pinpoint right now as the source of my fury. "You kept it secret."

"Again," she says with a hefty dose of sarcasm. "I was just a fuck to you for most of our time together. Why would I share?"

"You were not just a fuck, and you goddamn well know it," I growl.

"Do I?" she asks, and I can hear the near hysteria in her voice. She's really worked up, and I'm just... feeling betrayed.

Because Michelle betrayed me by not letting me know what was going on with her. She held something so deep and secretive she never gave me the opportunity to help her. She denied me my right to worry, and she demeaned my right as a husband to try to save her.

It appears to my psyche that Hannah is no different. She certainly had no problems handling the cancer on her own.

She's a secret keeper, too.

She doesn't need me or anyone it seems.

"Look," I say, the lack of strength in my voice showing I'm exhausted of this conversation. "If you don't mind, I think I'm going to head out. I can come back tomorrow and help finish up."

"No, that's okay," Hannah says, crossing her arms

over her chest and raising her chin. "I can manage on my own."

"You're good at that apparently," I can't help but remind her. I soften the sting of my words by leaning in and kissing her on the cheek. "Call me tomorrow if you want me to come help some more."

"Sure," she says, sounding as equally defeated as I am right now. She pats me on the chest before stepping back.

I let myself out. I don't look back at Hannah to see if she's watching me, but I think I can feel the weight of her stare.

It's accusing, and I feel wretched about it all.

But in the end, the only thing I can take with me as I make my way down the stairs to the parking lot is that Hannah confirmed a long-held belief of mine since Michelle died.

People can never truly know someone because it's dependent on that person to actually give the truth. And most people never do—at least not all of it.

## CHAPTER 26

# *Hannah*

DESPERATION DOESN'T LOOK good on me, and I know this. Yet, I find myself wanting to pathetically claw at Asher, because he's definitely slipping away.

It's been four days since I've seen him. As I walk out of the offices of Knight Investment Group, which is in the Symphony District of Las Vegas, I can't help the sense of foreboding that washes through me.

Asher was upset when he left my apartment Saturday night. While he offered to come back on Sunday to help with unpacking, his offer was lukewarm. I didn't ask him to come, and he was silent all day. It was lame, but I was waiting—hoping—he would just show up and everything would be okay.

Monday, I started my new job with his company. It's all right. I mean, I'm being paid a ridiculous amount of money to sit in a secretarial pool, but right now, it's the only choice I've got to pay the bills.

I'm not sure what I expected when it came to working for Asher's company. I'd realized it wouldn't be directly for him, or even remotely near him. As it turns out, his office is on the top floor of the three-story building he occupies, and I'm on the bottom. I haven't "bumped" into him once, but I haven't been trying either.

Sad to say, during the last three days, I've constantly poked my head over the cubicle I sat in, hoping to see him striding through the secretarial pool, intent on finding me.

Never happened.

It didn't mean things were radio silent. He texted me on Monday evening, said he'd gotten caught up in work, and wanted to know if I had gotten settled in at the new apartment. I texted back I had and thanked him for checking.

It was polite, standoffish, and calculated to see what he'd do.

His reply text was, *I'm glad.*

I wanted to throat punch him, but I also gave him the benefit of the doubt. I knew my brush with cancer freaked him out, but I still had hope he'd come around and realize it wasn't that big of a deal. Especially not with how well I've been doing.

With me now working a job away from Asher's apartment and having Hope almost full time, I knew our time together would be limited. But I truly expected more.

More contact, texts, calls, flowers… just something.

I reached out yesterday morning—Tuesday—with a text. I opted for light and sexy. *Any chance an employee could have lunch with the sexiest boss around?*

His text back felt like a sharp rebuke. *Sorry. Meetings all day.*

It was unlike the Asher I'd come to know. I have no doubt he had meetings all day, but the man I've been intimate with the last several weeks would have said something sexy in return. He would have told me a dirty fantasy or even offered another day we could see each other for lunch.

The writing was on the wall.

Except it's Wednesday and I still haven't fully accepted it.

When I reach my car, I put my purse on the hood and fish out my phone. I haven't heard from him at all today, and I just need to know where I stand. It's killing me and occupying way too many of my thoughts, this weird limbo he's put me in.

I type out a quick text, knowing he'll see it because his phone is always near him and he doesn't ignore it. Whether he'll reply is another matter.

*Any interest in dinner tonight? I can arrange a babysitter for Hope.*

I lean back against my car, staring at the phone with my stomach churning. To my surprise, the answer comes quickly, causing a jolt of excitement followed by a plummeting of my heart. *Can't. Have business dinner to attend.*

Pinpricks hit my eyes, and I blink stubbornly against them as I text back, *No worries.*

I hit send and then, because I need to know, I text again. One last, vain desperate attempt to know if we have a future together. *I've got to get a dress this week for the gala. Any interest in taking some time to help me pick one out?*

As I hit send, a wave of shame hits me over how pathetic I'm being. I should just come right out and ask him if we're over. Instead, I poke along the edges, terrified of the answer.

It doesn't come as quickly. In fact, it takes several minutes. I'm almost ready to give up and get in my car, knowing I'll have a date tonight with a pint of Ben and Jerry's at the least, when my phone chimes with his return text.

*I forgot to tell Christina I was bringing a date, and now all the tables are full. I won't be able to take you. I'm sorry.*

There was the slap in the face I'd been waiting for. The actual breakup he was too chicken shit to just come out and say.

It was over.

I've had tough times in my past. An upbringing rooted in poverty, a cheating husband, having cancer, a nasty divorce, and losing custody of Hope. Every fucking time, I raised my chin and chose to be stoic. I decided I was one tough bitch, and I could make it through. I'd watched my mom work her ass off and struggle to keep a roof over our heads and food in our bellies, and I'd been confident I could do anything if I put my mind to it.

Now... I can choose to do the same. I can let this experience with Asher be one of learning to compound my wisdom. Could decide to rejoice in the good times and be grateful for what I had.

Except right now, as the tears start to well up, I don't feel like being strong. Don't want to be tough and accepting. I don't want to change my life to cope with the letdown.

I want to fucking cry.

So I do.

For the first time that I can remember, I just decide to let my vulnerability have its moment in the spotlight and I let my emotions go.

Huddling down beside my car—with my arms wrapped hard around me because it hurts too much—I start to sob. No gentle lead up. No trying to hold it back. I let the dam burst, hoping it purges my pain with the saltiness licking down my face.

I moan, actually in physical pain, as I cry a river for a man who could have been my everything.

"Hannah?" I hear from above me. Through a haze of tears, I see my immediate supervisor, Kyla Wroth. She manages the secretarial pool and has been with Knight Investment Group for almost two decades. "Are you okay?"

She lowers herself in front of me, putting a hand on my knee with a worried expression on her face. "What happened?"

I dash the tears away with the back of my hand, sucking in a huge breath as I stand up. She follows along with me.

"I'm fine," I say in a quivery voice, shoving my phone back in my purse. "Just got some bad news."

"Is it something I can help you with?" she asks. While I've only known her for three days, I'm touched with her motherly concern. She has been brisk and polite at work, clearly not wanting to ever blur the lines between superior and subordinate. But right now, she looks like she just wants to grab me into a hard hug.

I finally lift my chin and put on a brave smile, once again wiping at my cheeks to catch a few stray tears. I'm proud at the strength behind my words. "No, really. I'm totally fine. Nothing like a good cry to make you feel better, right?"

She's not convinced. Her brow furrows, and she studies me carefully.

"Seriously," I assure her as I reach for my car door. "Thank you for your concern, but I'm really okay."

"Okay," she says hesitantly, but clearly not believing a word I just said. "If you need anything, I can give you my home phone number. You can call me if you'd like to talk."

"That's very sweet," I say. "But I'm good. I'll see you at work tomorrow, okay?"

"Sure," she says with a nod and a halfhearted smile.

I wait until she turns away from me before getting in my car. I turn it on, but don't leave right away. Instead, I pull my phone back out of my purse and I call my mom.

She answers right away. "Hey, honey."

"Hi, Mom," I say, and then my strength starts to crumble a little. I have to suck in a silent breath, then let it out just as quietly to get control of myself. "Um… I was thinking that Hope and I could maybe come visit for Thanksgiving next week."

"Oh, Hannah… that would be wonderful. Your brothers will be so excited, too."

"Awesome," I say in an overly bright voice. "I'll make the reservations tonight. I've got Thursday and Friday off. I think I'll try to find a flight out Wednesday night. Think someone can pick us up from the airport?"

We'd have to fly into Columbia, which was the closest airport to my hometown.

"Of course. We'll work it out. I'm just so thrilled. I can't remember the last time we all had Thanksgiving together."

"It will be great." And very much needed. I'm feeling so homesick right now.

We chat for a few more minutes, her basically wanting to know how the new job is going. She's been so thrilled over how my life has changed the last few weeks with Hope returning to me. While I've never let her directly in on just how hard things have been for me this past year, I know she still worries.

After I hang up, I take another deep breath and start the car. After I pick up Hope, we'll go out to dinner. I don't feel like cooking.

Or eating, to be honest. But I'll treat Hope to her favorite pizza.

Then, more than just making flight reservations, I need to figure out what to do with my life. I have what I think is a good idea—something that has always been on my radar of desires—and I'm hoping a few days back home next week and a lot of conversation with my mom will help put things into perspective. I still have a good chunk of the fifteen thousand Asher had given me weeks ago, so I have some breathing room if I decide to make a big change in my life.

# CHAPTER 27

## *Asher*

L EANING BACK IN my office chair, resting my elbows on the arms with my fingers steepled in contemplation, I stare out the window at the traffic below. I sent out an email about thirty minutes ago telling the employees their Thanksgiving holiday was starting early. I do it every year, so they were expecting it. It's a tradition my dad started, and I carried it on. Although we generally only give Thursday and Friday off for the holiday, we've always closed via "surprise" email to the company at noon on Wednesday.

Several of the executives and higher-level staff have stopped by my office. Poking their head in my open door and wishing me a happy Thanksgiving.

Fucking fat chance of that.

I suppose I could spend it at The Wicked Horse, but even I know that's not going to happen. Haven't been able to step foot in there since the last time Hannah and I went together as a couple.

Feeling brave, I went there Saturday night. I was supposed to be at the charity gala, but I chose not to go. Christina said she understood, but how could she really? She had no clue I hadn't gone because Hannah wasn't with me, nor that the whole fucked-up truth was that she wasn't with me was because I canceled the date. If Christina had known, she'd have thought I'd gone off the deep end.

So instead of getting into a tux for the gala, I put on a pair of faded jeans and a lightweight cashmere sweater and headed to the club.

I have no clue how long I stayed in my private parking spot in the garage. Eventually, there was a knock on my passenger window. It was Jerico bending over to look inside at me. I rolled the window down and lifted my chin. "What's up?"

Leaning his forearms on the door through the open window, he smirked. "What's up with me? What's up with you? You were sitting in your car when I got here almost two hours ago, and you're still sitting here now that I'm on my way out. Aren't you going in?"

I'd stared past him to the building that housed the Wicked Horse. Bringing my gaze back to Jerico, I lied to him. "Soon."

A hint of worry flashed in his eyes, but he knows me fairly well. I'd never share something personal with him, so he just nodded. "Have fun."

After I watched him leave, I put my car in reverse

and backed out. I headed home and went to bed with nothing but my memories of me and Hannah at The Wicked Horse. It didn't even get me aroused; it just made me melancholy as hell. I didn't try to chase it away, though. I welcomed the suffering because it's what I deserve after the way things ended with Hannah.

At least, I think they're ended. Neither of us has come out and said it, but the mere fact we've not spoken to each other by voice or text since I canceled our date for the gala is a good sign it's over.

My VP of marketing sticks her head in the door. "Have a great holiday, Asher."

"You, too, Vicki," I say with a smile.

When she leaves, I turn my gaze back out the window, letting my thoughts drift to Hannah again. She's really all I think about, and I've struggled to get through my workdays. I thought time and distance would make things easier, but they're getting worse.

I know Hannah thinks I'm upset because she held back information from me, and I'll admit I was a little perturbed when I learned she'd had cancer. But the truth is that I'm the world's biggest pussy because I pushed Hannah out of my life because she terrifies me now.

I see her as perhaps the best thing to ever happen to me in my life. If I were to fully embrace that, I predict catastrophic pain for me down the road if the cancer were to return and she died.

It's a long shot, I know that.

I researched the fuck out of Hodgkin's Lymphoma. Even called a doctor friend about it. It's true… if caught in its earliest stage, treatment is ninety-percent effective in curing the disease after the five-year mark. The chances of it recurring are nominal compared to winning the supposed greatest love of my life.

And yes… it's love.

Otherwise, why would I be this freaked out and afraid of that ten percent chance? I'm a man who has built his business successes on taking calculated risks. Why can't I take that same risk with my heart?

It's probably because I'm not sure I could survive losing Hannah. I think about us being together as a couple, sharing our lives and dreams with one another. I'd get to know Hope, and we'd grow to love one another. Perhaps Hannah and I would have children together. I know I'd have the best fucking partner I could ever dream of.

But what would happen if she died? Could I be strong and go on for our kids? Where would Hope go? Back to her father, which wouldn't seem fair to me because I would have grown to love her as my own.

Yes, these are the insane thoughts that have been circulating through my mind for over a week and a half.

Insane but also plausible, because I absolutely could see a future with Hannah prior to me finding out about her cancer. In fact, I'd say it was almost inevitable— that's how strongly I felt for her. I may not have told her that since I was growing to accept it myself, but it was there.

I'd opened the empty spaces inside of me to her, and she filled every fucking square inch.

I loved her.

Still love her.

Fuck.

When I hear a light knock on my door, I look up to see Kyla Wroth. She's the head of our resource department and Hannah's boss.

I smile and ask, "Headed out?"

"Not quite yet," she says as she steps in and closes the door behind her. I sit up straighter in my chair, because Kyla has been reporting to me on Hannah since she started work last week.

"Sit down," I say with a motion of my hand to one of the guest chairs.

She does, perching on the edge and folding her hands in her lap. She started out as a secretary here under my dad's watch and worked her way up the ladder until he put her in charge of our entire resource pool. She's smart, efficient, and most of all loyal to the company. That loyalty transferred from my dad to me when I became CEO.

"You asked me to keep a close eye on Hannah Madigan," she says, and I nod. I have and so far, her reports every few days by email have been benign. Hannah was doing well at work, exceeding expectations.

"Is everything okay?" There's no hiding the alarm in my voice.

Kyla shakes her head. "I don't think so. I didn't tell you last week because it seemed like a personal matter, and I wasn't sure it was relevant—"

"Is she sick?" I demand as I rise out of my chair.

Eyes rounding wide with unease, Kyla leans back in her chair. "Um… no. Not that I know of."

"Christ," I mutter as I scrub my fingers through my hair and plop back down in my chair. I give her a sheepish look. "I'm sorry."

Kyla purses her lips. "I really wasn't sure why you wanted me to keep an eye on her and it's none of my business, but now it's clear to me that you have feelings for her."

For a flash of a moment, I think to deny it, by why bother? Kyla has me pegged. Besides, there's no shame in caring for someone.

"Now I'm glad I decided to share this with you," she says with a tinge of censure in her tone. "Last week as I was coming out of work—actually a week ago today—I found Hannah crouched beside her car just sobbing her heart out."

"Fuck," I mutter. Last Wednesday after work. When I sent my last text to Hannah that I wasn't taking her to the gala. "Did she tell you what was wrong?"

"No," she replies briskly. "Dried her tears and put on a stiff upper lip."

"Okay?" I drawl expectantly, because there's clearly more to the story since that happened last week.

"She left a little bit ago after you sent the email about closing early," she continues. "I was walking around, encouraging some stragglers to leave, turning off lights, making sure computers were turned off, and I saw something on her desk."

"What?"

"It was on her printer, actually. A pamphlet to a college in South Carolina she must have printed out. It had an application with it to their business program. If I had to guess, Miss Madigan isn't going to be with us much longer. It appears she might be applying to college soon."

I stare at Kyla in shock, dread sinking in at what she's saying. Hannah is going to move halfway across the country?

"I'm not sure if you're understanding things," Kyla says, and I focus back in on her. Her words are pointed and challenging. "But I'm going to guess that Hannah was incredibly hurt last week by someone, and her only answer to it is to leave the area. It seems to me that if someone was having second thoughts about the rashness of their actions, they might want to take advantage of the early day off and purchase a plane ticket to South Carolina."

"South Carolina?" I ask, dumbfounded.

"Yes. Hannah's going there for the holidays with her

daughter."

She's going to South Carolina for Thanksgiving.

Looks like she's thinking about school there.

Hannah has moved on. Yet, I'm still left behind in this weird limbo, fighting my own feelings and fears.

"Jackie's already left," Kyla says. She's talking about my personal assistant. "Shall I make plane reservations for you?"

"Um… no," I tell her as I grab my phone off the desk. "I'll handle it myself. I have to call my sister first, though."

Kyla nods with a smile and stands from her seat. "Well, have a good holiday. Best of luck to you and Hannah."

"You too," I say without real thought, my mind already spinning out of control over how my life is getting ready to be decided very soon. But then I shake out of it and take a moment's pause. Looking at Kyla, I give her my heartfelt gratitude. "Thank you. For giving me a push. I needed the shake up."

"Anytime," she says with a grin.

Kyla leaves, shutting the door behind her. I dial my sister.

"Hey," she answers in a rushed sort of way that says she's busy and doesn't have a lot of time to talk. "I'm at the grocery store right now trying to buy last-minute shit I forgot for dinner tomorrow."

We're all planning to have dinner at her house tomorrow, Dad and Mandy included. It would have been interesting.

"I'm not going to make it tomorrow," I tell her, and I can almost hear her come to a dead stop in the grocery store.

"Why not?" She's immediately alarmed because she knows I've been all fucked in the head recently. While she said she understood I also know she was not happy over me backing out of the gala last Saturday, which was made clear when she showed up at my apartment Sunday morning to ream my ass out.

All it took was one look at me for her to realize I was suffering a heartbreak. I ended up telling her everything about Hannah.

She told me I was a dumbass. Warned me that I better figure that shit out soon, because Hannah wouldn't wait around.

"I'm flying to South Carolina," I tell her.

"What's in South Carolina?"

"Hannah," I say with a long exhale. "Going to try to fix this shit like you told me to."

"Well," she drawls. Since I can hear the squeak of the shopping cart wheels in the background, I can tell she's on the move again. "I suggest you do lots of groveling and apologizing."

"Duly noted," I say, although I figured that much out. "And I'm sorry I won't be there, especially about leaving you to deal with Dad alone."

Christina laughs. "No worries. You'll just owe me one."

"I owe you lots more than that," I say gently. "I love you, sis."

"Love you too, you big buffoon. Now go get Hannah."

"On it," I say and then disconnect the phone.

Next on the list… call the airlines and hope I can get a flight out of here today.

# CHAPTER 28

# *Hannah*

"HANNAH," MY MOM says from the stove where she's whisking the gravy. "Can you come grab the rolls out of the oven?"

"Sure," I reply. I leave my task of slicing the canned cranberry sauce, which is my favorite part of Thanksgiving, to do as she asked.

My mom moves to the side far enough I can open the oven door, but she still stirs the gravy so it doesn't clump. I use a towel to grab the pan of fresh rolls that are perfectly browned on top, placing it on the counter. After which, I transfer the hot rolls to a basket Mom had placed there with a decorative cloth napkin lining it.

"Mommy," Hope gasps as she rushes into the kitchen, holding up a quarter in her hand. "Look what Uncle Toby just pulled out of my ear. And I didn't even feel it."

"Ask him to look for more," I tell her with a laugh. "I've got to get your college fund started."

"Okay," she chirps and spins on her foot, running back into the living room.

"God, I love that kid." My mom chuckles.

"How could you not?" I ask with a grin.

I return to the cranberry sauce, and my mom carefully pours the gravy into a tureen.

"You know," she says thoughtfully, placing the empty pot back on the stove. She wipes her hands and turns to face me, "I really think moving back home is the best thing, baby."

Frank picked Hope and me up from the airport last night and brought us to Mom's house. She was waiting up for me. After I put a very sleepy Hope into the spare bedroom we'd share, we stayed up for about an hour talking. She made us tea and I poured my broken heart out to her, as well as my plan to move forward.

"Do you think Nelson will let you take Hope out of Nevada?" she asks worriedly.

"I don't know," I reply with equal worry. It's the only thing now that could screw up my plans. "He's not very invested in her emotionally. I've found out a lot of stuff since she came back to live with me, and he essentially ignored her or pawned her off on his flavor-of-the-month girlfriend. I can't imagine he'd put up much of a fight."

"What if you offered him financial incentive?" my mom asks slyly.

"Like what?"

"Waive child support," she suggests. "You could easily make that up by you and Hope living here with me rent free while you go to school."

"That's a thought," I muse as I finish the cranberry sauce. "But how about we put this out of our minds and eat?"

The gravy, rolls, and cranberry sauce were the last items to prepare. All the other food is already on the dining room table.

"Frank, Toby, Hope," my mom hollers as she takes her apron off. "Get in the dining room. We're ready to eat."

I hear some scuffling and something crashes, which tells me Toby and Frank are trying to beat each other through the door. Hope giggles, and my mom and I share a smile.

It's really, really good to be home.

Mom grabs the basket of rolls and the tureen of gravy, while I collect the plate of cranberry sauce. When we walk into the dining room, Toby and Hope are sitting on one side and Frank on the other. Frank helps clear some room for the rest of the food.

I take a seat next to Frank, and Mom sits at the end to my immediate right. She smiles at me, then looks around at her family collected together. It's been almost two years since I've been home, when Nelson, Hope, and I last came for Christmas. She's just as happy now as she was then to have her brood all under one roof.

Nelson, of course, seemed to hate every minute of it. He'd kept his face in his phone most of the time.

Spreading her arms, she holds a hand out to me and the other to Hope, who sits directly across from me. The circle is complete when I take Frank's hand, he takes Toby's, and Toby finishes it off by taking Hope's.

My mom bows her head and prays, "Dear Lord… thank you for the bounty you put before us and for keeping me from burning the gravy."

When Toby snorts, I open one eye and smirk across the table at him.

A glance at my mom shows an amused smile on her face as she continues. "But mostly, thank you for bringing Hannah and Hope home, so I have all my youngins with me. You've made this woman mighty happy, and I'll put extra money in the church basket on Sunday. Amen."

"Amen," we all chorus and break apart, all of us reaching for the nearest bowl in front of us. I scoop out some green bean casserole while Frank takes three slices of the freshly carved turkey. Toby puts a glob of gooey mac and cheese on Hope's plate, then a bigger one on his own.

Just as I'm reaching for the turkey, there's a knock on the door.

"I'll get it," Toby says as he pushes out of his chair, licking a piece of cheese off his thumb.

"Hope," I say as I stab a piece of turkey for her.

"Hold your plate out for me."

She does, and I deposit the meat as I ask, "Want some green bean casserole?"

My daughter wrinkles her nose with a grimace. She hates almost all vegetables.

"Corn?" I ask.

She hesitates and nods. I give her a small spoonful because I know she won't eat all of it.

Just as I'm getting ready to put some corn on my plate, Toby walks into the dining room with someone following him.

He steps to the side and there's Asher Knight, staring right at me.

"What are you doing here?" I gasp, and the table goes silent. All eyes turn to Asher.

Not answering me directly, he moves to my mother, sticking his hand out. "Sorry for the intrusion. I'm Asher Knight, and I'm a friend of Hannah's. You must be her mother, Carol."

"Pleased to meet you," my mom says politely, but there's no mistaking the coolness in her tone. While I would never in a million years let her know how our relationship started, I didn't spare her any details on how we broke up. "Would you like to join us?"

"Um… no, but thank you," Asher says politely, and then moves around the table with his eyes on Frank. He sticks his hand out and Frank takes it, looking utterly confused as they shake. "You must be Frank. Hannah's told me a lot about you."

"Good to meet you," my brother replies before turning questioning eyes to me.

I shrug as I stare at Asher. His gaze comes to mine, and I'm shocked when he says, "I need to talk to Hope for a minute. You can be there, too, of course."

My head snaps Hope's way. She's studying Asher with narrowed eyes. He gives her his attention and says with a smile, "Hey, kiddo. Can we talk?"

Hope looks to me. I don't know what type of game he's playing, but I intend to figure it out. I stand up from my chair. "Let's go outside, because this is getting awkward."

"Or would you rather me and Toby escort him out for you?" Frank says ominously, now having figured out there's something bad between us.

"I got it," I tell my brother with a pat to his shoulder. I'm surprised he doesn't crack his knuckles while he glares at Asher.

Asher, on the other hand, looks confidently back at my brother. He's not intimidated in the least.

I walk around the table, going the opposite way around so I don't have to brush past Asher. I'm afraid what might happen if we make contact. I can already feel the thickness of the air around us.

When I hold my hand out to Hope, she takes it and follows me out of the dining room, into the foyer, and out the front door. It's a relatively mild day for a late

November in the south, but still brisk enough we need to wear long sleeves. I'm wearing a flannel shirt and jeans. Hope's got on a fuzzy pink sweater and pink corduroys. If asked, she'd say in an exaggerated southern voice ala *Steel Magnolias*, "Pink is my signature color."

I turn around and find Asher right behind us, pulling the front door behind him. He looks at me, to Hope, and then back to me again. He tips his head in Hope's direction and asks me, "Do you mind?"

*Do I mind you talking to my daughter before you say a word to me?* I am intrigued enough not to.

"Sure," I say magnanimously.

Asher smiles at Hope, who is staring at him with wide eyes. He squats down in front of my daughter to get eye level with her, and I try not to notice how well his muscular legs fill out the denim he's wearing. No matter how mad or upset I am with him, I'll always be ridiculously attracted to his ass.

Asher gives a little cough to clear his throat, and then just lays it on the line to my daughter. "Hope… I hurt your mommy pretty bad. Honestly, I was a jerk to her, and there's no excuse for it. I'm here to apologize to her and ask her to give me another chance, but first I need to ask you if that's okay with you. Because without your approval, I know I'll never stand a chance with her because you're the most important thing in her life."

I have no clue if those words have any effect on my kid, but damn if they don't hit me deep and true, right in the center of my chest.

I wait anxiously as I watch Hope, because if she says "no," then it's absolutely over. No matter if I love this man or not, Hope has to accept him.

Of course, I'm not sure she really understands anything. She had asked me one day last week if we were still going to Disneyland with Asher. If she'd noticed I'd been in a funk over him, she never said. She's five years old and focused on Mickey Mouse.

I apologized and told her it wasn't going to happen. She asked, "Why?"

And I couldn't exactly tell her. All I could say is, "I don't know, honey. But I'm not seeing him anymore."

Hope glances up at me as if seeking permission to even give Asher the time of day. I don't give her any encouragement, just a soft smile that I hope conveys she should do what's in her heart.

She turns to Asher, her voice earnest and deliberate. "I want my Mommy to be happy."

I'm amazed by my kid's savvy understanding of something that should be beyond her grasp. She doesn't answer him directly. Doesn't say she's giving him another chance, but rather telling him the standard he must meet to gain her approval.

And then amazingly, she puts the ball in his court. "I'm hungry and going to go eat now."

Asher is speechless. He just watches her walk inside, an awed expression on his face. When the door closes, he stands up.

I take a few steps back to lean against the post that connects the porch railing. Pushing my hands down into my pockets, I stare at him and wait.

He throws a thumb toward the door where Hope just disappeared. "Your kid is pretty amazing."

"I know," I say with a smug smile. She's the best.

Asher stares out across the field that's barren now but usually filled with tobacco in the summers. My mom's house is in the "country" surrounded by farmland on three sides and forest on the other.

He then moves to the post opposite of me and leans back against it. He mimics me by shoving his hands down into his pockets.

This tells me several things. First, he's being cautious with me because the Asher I know would just demand I take him back and would probably kiss me to put me under his thrall. That also shows respect for me, since he's putting distance between us so I can think for myself.

"Are you really thinking of moving back here and going to school?" he asks.

I blink at him in surprise, somewhat impressed and offended at the same time. "How do you know that?"

"Kyla Wroth saw the pamphlet and application on your printer. I didn't know you were interested in college."

"There's a lot you don't know about me, Asher. We

haven't really spent a lot of quality time talking."

Fucking definitely. The man knows my body better than I do.

My mind, my ambitions… not so much.

"I figured out why you want to leave. You have no security in Vegas." His expression is apologetic. "I took that away from you, I realize that. You've probably been wondering when the rug might get pulled out from under you, working for my company and me just cutting things off. Wondering every night if you'd still have that job the next morning. I get it."

Okay… maybe he knows me a little better than I give him credit for.

"But you're also running away from me and a broken heart," he says, his voice now gritty with determination. "I'm here to fix that if you let me."

# CHAPTER 29

## *Asher*

M Y HEART BLEEDS for Hannah. I'm not making things easier, even though I'm trying. I'll eventually right my wrongs, but I need to let Hannah get there on her own steam and resolve.

"What makes you think I'm heartbroken over you?" she asks defiantly.

"I guess I don't," I admit truthfully. "I guess I'm just hoping. But I'm certain you're pissed, and you have every right to be."

Hannah's cheeks turn pink, as if I'd just discovered a dirty secret about her. She'd like me to believe she's not mad, as if I'm not worth the effort. But I refuse to believe that.

"It doesn't matter," she says primly.

"It does. I want to make it right."

"Why?" she retorts angrily, pushing off from the post and advancing toward me. She goes to her tiptoes and gets right in my face. I glance over her shoulder to the dining room window to see both her brothers' faces there, spying on us. They pull quickly back, and my attention goes to their sister when she pokes me in the chest. "Why do you want to make it right? Why are you here?"

"Because—"

"You owe me nothing. I am not your problem or your concern."

"You are—"

"I'm not," she growls, cutting me off and speaking right over me. "You made that clear when you didn't even have the balls to tell me we were over."

"I didn't know—"

Once again, she shuts my explanations down. "You were a lame-ass for canceling our date to the gala so you wouldn't have to be around me."

"Hannah," I warn.

"All because you thought I was hiding something from you. That I was being disingenuous, which is the most insulting thing—"

If she wanted to poke the bear, she succeeded, because now my anger flares. "Goddamn it, Hannah," I yell. "I was terrified you were going to fucking die."

Her mouth snaps shut, and she looks unsure of herself. However, her glare is still there.

She stays quiet, though, and listens.

I bring my hands to her shoulders, hating the way she stiffens slightly from my touch. I gentle my voice.

"I've lost someone I've loved before, and I survived it. But I know without a doubt I can't survive losing you."

Hannah's chin jerks inward with disbelief. "Of course you can. You're the strongest person I know."

I disregard that, because I feel like a fucking pussy with my fears. Instead, I tell her, "I need you to know I didn't back away from you because I was mad you didn't tell me about the cancer. It was purely out of fear that I was setting myself up for a potential catastrophic pain I wouldn't survive. And for the record, it's not that I didn't have the balls to break things off with you. It's sort of more like I was stalling until I could figure shit out. It wasn't as permanent in my mind if I just stopped communicating as it would be if I broke it off in no uncertain terms."

Hannah pulls back from me, crossing her arms over her chest almost protectively. "No. You were done. Canceling our date to the gala was a very clear message."

"There was no date to the gala." Her eyes widen with incredulity, so I rush to explain. "I didn't go. If I couldn't have you by my side, I didn't want to go. But I didn't know how to overcome the fear to have you by my side. My sister was pissed. She still hasn't really forgiven me for what I did to you or for missing the gala."

Hannah gives me a censuring look. "I can't believe you didn't go. That was your mother's pet project. I know how important it is to you. To Christina."

"Very important," I reiterate. "But I'm telling you,

Hannah. I was fucked in the head about all this."

She just watches me, her face a mask of confusion.

I'm struggling to make it clear to her, but I can't give up. I step into her, back her into the porch post, and take her hands in mine. "Hannah… my wife died and there was nothing I could do about it. It was devastating, no doubt, and I really struggled over the lack of control I had in the situation. So here comes this woman who captivates me in a way I've never known, and she made me forget that pain. She made me want to feel again."

"That woman would be me, right?" she asks softly, a small smile to her mouth. The first sign I've seen that I'm getting through.

"That would be you," I assure her. "And when I realized you could potentially die on me—after I'd just realized I'd fallen in love with you—I just couldn't rationally process the emotions I felt. I didn't want to fall in love again. I didn't want to set myself up for hurt again. And yet, you were the ultimate prize. You were in reach, and now there's a huge canyon between us filled with fear and doubt. So I backed off. Put you at arm's length while I tried to process things."

Hannah's head turns, and her gaze drifts out across the front yard. It's as if she's afraid to believe what I'm saying.

I bring a hand to her face, grip her jaw gently, and turn her back to me. "It's not easy for me to admit a weakness, Hannah. But I'm here telling you that it was fear of losing someone I'd fallen in love with that made me do the stupid things I've done. It was incredibly idiotic of me to think that perhaps if I broke things off now, when I'd just fallen in love with you, it wouldn't hurt as bad as if I were more deeply in love with you and you died on me."

"I'm not going to die," she asserts stubbornly.

"I don't know that," I return softly. "And it's my burden to bear. To try to figure out how to fucking cope with it. It's up to me to decide if I'm strong enough to give up control of my fate and future."

Hannah's head tilts. "And how do you get there?"

"By accepting that you're my soul mate." I dip my head, get closer to her. "By taking the risk and putting myself out there."

"And you're ready for that?"

I smile. "I didn't know I was until Kyla told me about that college pamphlet. Like I said… I didn't have the guts to call it over, because I was still trying to figure shit out. But knowing that you were making plans to move on, well… I knew without a doubt I was ready for it. I tried to hop a plane yesterday afternoon, but everything was fucking booked. This was the earliest I could get here."

Hannah graces me with a small smile.

A true smile that doesn't look forced or pained.

It gives me hope.

I step back from her. "I'm going to let you get back

to your family dinner. I'm staying at the Eastover Inn in town. Maybe we could talk again over breakfast or something."

I turn to the porch, waiting for her to stop me.

To give me some sign she's heard what I've said—has realized that even dumbasses can be forgiven their weaknesses.

I make it to the third step down when the front door opens. It's not Hannah who stops me; it's her mother. "Wait a minute."

Turning around, I find her standing there with her hand on Hope's shoulder. Hope's expression is uncertain.

"Hope needs to talk to you again," she says from the doorway before giving a little nudge to her granddaughter.

Hannah watches carefully, not saying a word.

Hope inches out, darting a glance at her mom. It's a silent question if it's okay that she interferes in our discussion.

"What's up, baby?" Hannah asks her.

She seems unsure, lowering her gaze shyly. Hannah raises her eyebrow at her mom, who explains, "We were all inside talking about um… you two… and Hope had some questions."

"Ask away, kiddo," I say as I come back onto the porch. Once again, I squat down to get on eye level with her.

Another glance at her mom, who reassures her, "It's okay, honey."

Hope turns to me, clasping her hands in front of her. "Do you love my mommy?"

"I do," I tell her with no room in my tone for uncertainty by anyone. "More than anything I've ever loved before."

I hear Hannah gasp, because while we just had a deep discussion of feelings, fears, and emotions, I didn't come right out and tell her that.

Keeping my gaze on Hope, I patiently wait for any other questions.

I go completely hot under the collar when she asks bluntly, "Are you going to marry her?"

My gaze flicks up to Hannah, who has gone pale, before I focus back on Hope. "If your mom loves me the way I love her, then yes... without a doubt I would."

Something sly flits across Hope's face, and I realize I might be getting played here.

"If you get married," she says deliberately, "can I have a brother or a sister?"

What the fuck? This kid is beyond stinking smart and totally manipulative, in the absolute best of ways.

"Um... yeah," I say without really thinking too much about it.

"One of each would be great," she replies with a sharp nod of her head. She then turns to Hannah, and I about lose my shit when she holds her thumb up. "If he makes you happy, Mommy, then I think he's okay to keep around."

Hannah chokes back a laugh, covering her mouth with her hand to hide her grin.

"Okay, Hope… let's get back inside," Carol says, shooting first me a smirk, then Hannah an amused grin.

After they're gone and the door closes, Hannah and I are once again facing each other on the porch. There's a slightly awkward silence before Hannah asks, "You'd really give Hope a brother and a sister?"

"You make it sound like I'm just going out to buy one at the local mall or something," I chide. "You'd have to be an integral part of that decision."

Hannah slaps lightly at my chest. "You know what I mean."

I grab her hand, tug her into me. She tries to pull back, but I bring my other hand to her lower back to hold her against me. "If I wasn't clear with your daughter, let me be now with you. I love you. More than anything I've ever loved before or will ever love again. If you say yes, I'd marry you today. I would relish practicing making babies with you. When you're ready, I'd love to make as many as you want. I have a feeling Hope would be even happier with more than two. And although I didn't say it to her just then, I'll say it to you now so you have no fucking doubt about it—I'll love Hope as my own, too. Now, I've done a fuck of a lot of talking and laid my entire soul bare to you. Yet, I have no clue what you're thinking or if you even have a slight fondness for me. So I'm going to leave, head back to my motel, and if you—"

It's as far as I get before Hannah is throwing her arms around my neck and pulling me down for a hard, bruising kiss. I've never felt such utter relief in my entire life.

I kiss her back, bringing a hand to her neck and bending her backward. My gaze cuts to the window to see her mom, both brothers, and her daughter watching us.

I hastily pull her upright, sadly taking my mouth from hers.

Hannah's eyes are sparkling, incandescent with something I've never quite seen before.

Then she says the words that make me understand what I'm seeing. "I love you, Asher. And while you hurt me terribly, I can understand where your fear was coming from."

"Thank fuck," I mutter. I kiss her again, except this time gently and much more chastely since we're being watched. I pull back again. "I love you so much, Hannah."

Then I'm pulling her into an embrace once more. As I hold her, I make a vow I will never, ever let her go. I choose to let go of the worry and doubt over our future, knowing that each day I have with her in the future will be the best day I've ever had, and that's not something I could ever turn my back on. It's the greatest kind of risk.

"Come on inside and let's get you a plate," she says as she takes my hand and leads me to the door. "Then you have cleanup duty with my brothers while Mom and I relax since we did all the cooking."

"Deal," I say with a broad smile as we both see her family scramble away from the window.

Her family that is soon to be my family as well—I'm sure of it.

# EPILOGUE

## *Hannah*

THE GRAND BALLROOM at the Mandarin Oriental is sparkling with wealth and glamour this evening. Round tables that seat ten are overflowing with fine china, crystal, and silver. I thought Hope would be bored to death, but she seems to be enjoying it, I think as dazzled as I've been from all the diamonds flashing on the women and their fancy ballgowns.

The Dorothy Knight Charity Extravaganza for the Benefit of Children's Hospital is wrapping up, once again having raised thousands and thousands of dollars from all these wealthy people in attendance.

It was important to Asher that both Hope and I attend with him. He still feels guilty for missing it last year when he and I were... well, going through our thing. Of course, I wouldn't miss it, and Hope was more than willing to go when Asher bought her the pink satin and tulle gown she's wearing tonight.

Even in first grade, pink is still her signature color.

This evening, we dined on Kobe beef and Maine lobster with lots of expensive champagne. Not sure how she pulled it off, but Christina managed to have pizza served to Hope, which totally made her night.

Asher is now striding on stage to give the closing remarks, a spotlight following him. In addition to the thousand-dollar-a-plate ticket the people paid to get in, an all-night auctioneer has been showcasing expensive donated items while managing the excitement of competing bids as the numbers raised to staggering numbers.

At one point, Christina leaned over to whisper to me, "You know that Chihuly vase you broke of Asher's?"

I nodded, trying not to fondly smile over it since my breaking it is what led me to the love of my life.

"He bought it at the gala the year before," she said with a smirk.

"Money well spent," I replied with a grin. It also explained why his starkly barren interior of an apartment was graced with such a colorful object. It seemed so "anti" Asher.

Over the past year, we've been on a few shopping trips where he's let me pick out some stuff to brighten up his place. A few pieces of artwork, some colorful pillows, and even a pretty green-and-blue duvet cover for the master bedroom. I don't get to sleep there except the nights Nelson has Hope, but it made me feel good he wanted my touch there.

Asher gives a tap to the microphone before putting his forearms on the podium where he casually leans. He beams out at the crowd and says, "Folks… we've come to the end of the night, and I want to report that we've raised a grand total of $268,000 for Children's Hospital."

The room erupts into thunderous applause.

Asher waits for it to die a little and adds, "And because it drives me nuts to see such an odd figure, I'm going to donate another thirty-two thousand dollars to make it an even $300,000."

There's more applause, and Hope grins at me as she claps enthusiastically. She and Asher have grown close this past year. Tonight, he's absolutely walking on water in her eyes.

He's pretty fine in my eyes, too. Sometimes I think it's impossible for me to be more attracted to him than I already am, but damn… him in that tuxedo is driving me crazy. He's going to stay the night at my apartment tonight, and I hope to hell I can keep it quiet.

"I want to thank my sister, Christina, for perfectly organizing this event year after year. She outdoes herself every time." Asher pauses to search out our table, which is right in front of the stage. He smiles at Christina. "I'm so proud of you, sis, and you truly are the best of us Knights."

This time, the applause is almost deafening, a testament to how much Christina is revered in this wealthy community for her charitable efforts. She stands and waves, the spotlight briefly swinging to her.

It's touching when her father stands as well, overtly clapping for her like he's her biggest champion. His wife, Mandy, is beside him, also giving praise to Christina with her own effusive applause.

Carlton and Mandy have been a pleasant twist to Asher's life this past year. When his father married Mandy, thirty-two years his junior, he became a changed man. She's a lovely woman who genuinely loves Carlton. He rarely comes into the offices to look over Asher's shoulder anymore, content to concede the entire business to his son. He and Mandy instead travel the world. When they're in Vegas, they are very present in his kids' lives. I think he might have some making up to do, but I've enjoyed getting to know them. Best of all, they spoil Hope as if she were actually their grandchild, so they're fairly esteemed in my book.

The applause dies down and the spotlight swings from Christina back to Asher on stage. God, he's so handsome. And just such a good man. I'm very aware of how blessed I am that he decided to take a chance on me and on love. Since I returned with him to Vegas after Thanksgiving last year, I have not regretted a single second I've spent with him.

My life has become almost magical. I'm in love with the best man I've ever known. I work part time for his company, still in the secretarial pool since it's all I'm really qualified for, but I also go to school part time where I'm working toward a general business degree. Asher wanted to pay my tuition so I could go full time and be done faster, but I think I finally made him understand there are some things I just need to do for myself.

I don't always need my Knight rushing in to save me.

I still live in my apartment with Hope, much to Asher's consternation, although he will stay some nights with us. At least once a day, he tries to talk me into us moving in with him. He's resorted to begging, but I've held out. While we're dating, I would like us to have separate residences. It's not really part of a moral compass I'd like to instill in my daughter so much as I want to show her that it's cool to be an independent woman.

Of course, no telling how long having our own residences will last. Since coming back to Vegas last year with Asher, there's been no proposal or talk of marriage, but that was at my insistence. Even though he made it clear he wanted to marry me and would have gladly taken me to a justice of the peace back in South Carolina, I asked if we could take it a bit slow.

Not that I had any doubts about us, but because I wanted to show Hope it's always good to take things slowly—to make sure that all of our dreams are being reached in the right way. While I'd kill to sleep by my man every night, I also know that our growth together has become so solid I won't hesitate when he finally pops the question.

Admittedly, there's a part of me that was a little hesitant early on. I take great care to give validation to the fears Asher has about me dying. While I'm at peace with my diagnosis and prognosis, he still struggles. This is emphasized if I get sick. He doesn't necessarily freak out, but he goes way overboard in his zeal to take care of me. The last time I got a sniffle, he ran to the drugstore and brought back thirteen different over-the-counter medicines for me to try.

God, I love him for it, too.

And I know he's the only one for me. Next to Hope, he's the greatest love of my life. As my love for him deepened over this year, I had more of an appreciation of how Asher freaked out at the thought of my cancer recurring. When I reversed roles, the thought of me ever losing him is so painful I do question how I would have the strength to go on. Of course I would… for Hope. But I sure as hell have a greater appreciation for his fears about me.

"There is one more thing I'd like to say before we call it a night," Asher says into the microphone. The room goes completely silent. "I want to speak directly to my love, Hannah Madigan."

The spotlight swings to me. I feel like the proverbial deer frozen in place as I stare up at Asher. He smiles casually back at me. From my right, Hope giggles. I tear my eyes from him to my daughter to mouth, "What's going on?"

Hope grins and shrugs.

Slowly turning my attention back to Asher, I almost pass out as he reaches into his pocket and pulls out a black velvet box.

There are oohs and ahhs, along with a smattering of applause. He holds it up high for everyone to see. "That's right, folks. This is exactly what you think it is."

There's more clapping and one person hollers out, "Say yes. You know that rock has to be massive."

There's laughter everywhere, and Asher gestures with his hand for people to settle down. His eyes come back to me and while he's speaking to the crowd, it feels like he's only talking to me. "My woman is cautious and wanted to take our relationship slow. I agreed to it because there isn't anything I wouldn't give this amazing lady."

My heart starts beating so hard I'm afraid I'm going to pass out. If that doesn't happen, I'm getting so melty-swoony from the way he's speaking to me that I might just flop out of my chair.

I hold my breath as he continues. "Hannah... I've respected that you wanted to move slowly but we've been together over a year, and Hope and I have been talking."

At that, my breath comes rushing out and I snap my attention to my daughter once again, who is still giggling like a damn fool.

"Hope is Hannah's beautiful daughter," he tells the crowd as the spotlight illuminates us both. "And like I said... we've been talking. And we think it's way past time that we move this to the next level."

I can't help but smile, shaking my head in both embarrassment and total awe that Asher's making such a spectacle of himself. I guess he figures if he puts a spotlight on me, I can't say no.

"Hope," Asher booms into the microphone. "Grab your mom and get her up here for me."

People start cheering. There are whistles as my daughter grabs my hand and pulls me from my seat. I pick up my dress so I don't trip on the hem, then follow my daughter as she leads me onto the stage with Asher.

When I reach him, I give him a look that says I'm going to kill him later for doing this to me in public. In reality, though, I'm going to show him my love and appreciation—probably with my mouth on his cock.

Asher grins at me, opens the box, and holds the ring out for me to inspect. It's exquisite and monstrous, and it's going to totally weigh my hand down.

"Hope helped me pick it out so it's totally kid approved," Asher leans toward the microphone to tell the crowd. They roar with approval.

But then Asher steps away from the podium and goes to one knee before me. After giving a quick wink to Hope, he pulls the ring from the box and slides it onto my finger. He then holds my hand tight to his chest.

Looking up at me, he says, "Hannah... I love you. You are my everything. You are woven so deeply into the fabric of my soul that I don't know where I end and you start. I don't want to know, either. I like the way you make me feel alive and whole and so very much loved. I'll give the same back to you all the days of your life if you'll have me. I want you and Hope by my side, so please stop torturing me and agree to be my wife."

My head is bobbing up and down, a resounding yes before he even finishes, and the crowd stands and starts clapping for our engagement.

I crook the finger on my other hand, gesturing for Asher to stand. He needs to make it fast because I demand to be kissed.

My man does not disappoint, giving me a searing kiss that makes me dizzy. He then turns to the microphone and says, "Thank you, everyone, for attending and for your generous donations. Goodnight."

With that, Asher takes both mine and Hope's hands and leads us off the stage. He pulls us into the corner and puts his back to the rest of the room, a clear sign he wants some privacy with us.

I'm stunned when he pulls another box from inside his jacket. It's another ring box.

Asher then kneels in front of Hope, opening the box for her to see inside. "Hope... I got a promise ring for you, and it is to show my commitment to love you just as much as I love your mother. I want you to know that my place is never between you and your mom, but rather to be near you both to catch you if you stumble."

It's at this point I lose it. Tears start to spill down my cheeks. Hope looks at Asher so solemnly that it's clear he holds a big part of her heart. He takes the ring, a delicate band of platinum set with pink stones that I would hazard to guess are diamonds. It's a ridiculously pricey piece of jewelry for a six-year-old, yet I wouldn't expect anything else of Asher.

Hope gives him a big hug, and I wipe my tears before I turn into a raccoon.

Christina comes up and grabs my hand, quickly oohs and aahs over my diamond, and then drops it. "Okay... you guys have to leave. You're running late. Limo is in front of the hotel."

"Limo?" I ask curiously, and she just shrugs before giving me a quick hug and dashing off. I turn to Asher. "Limo?"

He stands up, still holding Hope's hand in his. "Oh, yeah... one more surprise for you ladies. We're getting in a limo right now and heading straight to the airport, where we'll take a private jet t-o-o-o...."

He glances at Hope, pausing an evilly long time before declaring, "Disney World!"

Hope shrieks, throwing herself at Asher so hard he almost falls over. She hugs his legs tightly with her eyes screwed up. It's been her dream to go there. Of course, Asher's taken us both to Disneyland twice this year for weekend trips, but her dream trip is to Disney World in

Orlando, Florida.

Asher continues like a game show announcer in his enthusiasm. He claps his hands together and rubs them. "That's right, ladies. Six wonderful nights at the Grand Floridian Hotel, where we'll enjoy fine dining at night while we explore all the parks there by day."

"Oh my God," Hope exclaims as she jumps up and down. "Let's go. Let's go."

Asher laughs and takes her hand, offering his other to me. We start to stroll out of the ballroom.

I lean over and whisper, "You don't have to buy her love, you know. She loves you just as you are."

"Oh, I know," he says with a sly twinkle in his eye. "This isn't about buying her love. It's about putting our wedding together. Your mom and brothers will meet us there. I've got a pastor on tap to marry us. Even hired a horse and carriage to bring my Cinderella to me. So really, this is our honeymoon, Hannah. Your mom and brothers can take Hope hopping around all the parks while you and I consummate our marriage all day, every day."

I stare at him, completely agog over his foresight.

Doubt flits across his face. "Unless this is moving too fast. We can do the wedding when you're ready."

Furiously shaking my head, I smile. "No. It's perfect. You're perfect. I'm so ready to be your wife, Asher. Let's do it."

"Let's do it," he agrees. And then he leads his girls away to the start of our new future together as a family.

Want more Wicked Horse Vegas? GO HERE to see all of the sinfully sexy standalones available in the Wicked Horse Vegas series.

sawyerbennett.com/bookstore/the-wicked-horse-vegas-series

Go here to see other works by Sawyer Bennett:

https://sawyerbennett.com/bookshop

Don't miss another new release by Sawyer Bennett!!! Sign up for her newsletter and keep up to date on new releases, giveaways, book reviews and so much more.

https://sawyerbennett.com/signup

## Connect with Sawyer online:

Website: sawyerbennett.com

Twitter: twitter.com/bennettbooks

Facebook: facebook.com/bennettbooks

Instagram: instagram.com/sawyerbennett123

Book+Main Bites:

bookandmainbites.com/sawyerbennett

Goodreads: goodreads.com/Sawyer_Bennett

Amazon: amazon.com/author/sawyerbennett

BookBub: bookbub.com/authors/sawyer-bennett

# About the Author

Since the release of her debut contemporary romance novel, Off Sides, in January 2013, Sawyer Bennett has released multiple books, many of which have appeared on the New York Times, USA Today and Wall Street Journal bestseller lists.

A reformed trial lawyer from North Carolina, Sawyer uses real life experience to create relatable, sexy stories that appeal to a wide array of readers. From new adult to erotic contemporary romance, Sawyer writes something for just about everyone.

Sawyer likes her Bloody Marys strong, her martinis dirty, and her heroes a combination of the two. When not bringing fictional romance to life, Sawyer is a chauffeur, stylist, chef, maid, and personal assistant to a very active daughter, as well as full-time servant to her adorably naughty dogs. She believes in the good of others, and that a bad day can be cured with a great work-out, cake, or even better, both.

Sawyer also writes general and women's fiction under the pen name S. Bennett and sweet romance under the name Juliette Poe.

Made in the USA
Middletown, DE
26 August 2019